Good-bye, Glamour Girl

Good-bye, Glamour Girl

by Erika Tamar

J.B. LIPPINCOTT   NEW YORK

Library of Congress Cataloging in Publication Data
Tamar, Erika.
Good-bye, glamour girl.

Summary: When Liesl, a Jewish refugee from Nazi-
occupied Vienna, arrives in New York, she is determined
to leave her European heritage behind and become as all-
American, glamourous, and famous as her idol, the film
star Rita Hayworth.
[1. Jews—Fiction. 2. New York (N.Y.)—Fiction.
3. World War, 1939–1945—United States—Fiction]
I. Title.
PZ7.T159Go 1984   [Fic]   83-49493
ISBN 0-397-32087-6
ISBN 0-397-32088-4 (lib. bdg.)

For my mother and in memory of my father

I

There are some things where you know just exactly
how they started. I mean, you can point at that
very minute and examine it and say, "Right here,
here's where it started." It was like that with me and
Rita Hayworth.

Then there are things that sneak up on you a little
at a time. Like me and Billy Laramie. I can't even
remember the first time I ever saw him.

The Rita Hayworth part is easier.

I was on the second floor of Wertheimer's on 181st
Street. The bottom floor was ladies' housedresses and
stuff like that, nothing interesting, but the second
floor had toys in the back. There was a miniature dress
shop with teeny hangers and a make-believe glass window, and I knew we couldn't afford anything like that,
but I liked to go to visit it. I must have liked it a lot,

because it was a long ten blocks from 191st Street. Anyway, at the top of the stairs, right in the middle of the nightgown counter, in a silver frame, was a photograph of a lady kneeling. She was wearing a nightgown, and you could tell, even in black and white, that it was silky, some kind of satin, and her skin was shining just a little bit, like some kind of satin, too, and her hair was real long and in soft curls. Her mouth was perfectly formed in a secret smile, and I didn't know any real person could look that beautiful. I used to like the fairy tales where the princess was the most beautiful in the whole world. But this was a photograph, and I didn't know any real person could look like that. There was a name all the way down on the bottom, in little print: RITA HAYWORTH.

The most important thing was that her nose didn't turn up at all, and she was beautiful anyway. See, all the really pretty Irish girls in the neighborhood had those little Irish upturned noses. Sometimes I'd hold the tip of my nose up with my finger for a long time, hoping maybe I could train it that way. You know, the way you train your hair to part a certain way.

I still had that picture in my head when I got to 191st Street and St. Nicholas Avenue and cut through the subway arcade. Our subway wasn't the regular kind, it wasn't just stairs going down. The IRT subway station at 191st Street happened to be the very deepest in all of New York City. I liked that a lot. I liked things that were the *most* of something. Anyway, there were elevators with elevator operators and creaky iron gates, and there were two entrances with a passageway in between. There was always a damp metal smell. On one side were the barbershop and Jackandandy's candy store, and on the other was the Chinese laundry. I can almost hear Billy Laramie saying, "So what's that got to do with Rita Hayworth?" Billy used to say I talked too much and I'd go on and on from one subject to another, and I guess he was right. Sometimes my mind raced ahead of me and I talked too fast. Okay. I liked to cut through the subway arcade because that way I could avoid the bar and grill on the corner. I worried that some fighting drunk would come reeling out just as I was passing by and bump into me and get mad. That's because one time I was riding in the subway with my mother and father and sister, Hedi, and there were three sailors who were very drunk. A man said, "If you're drunk, take off your uniform," and they got mad and started fighting with him. They were standing up on the seats and jumping off at him and swinging from the overhead straps, and it was very scary. They were jumping all over the place, like they thought they were in the war, fighting in the Pacific jungles or something.

Anyway, that's why I cut through the arcade and passed by Jackandandy's. I looked at the magazines out in front and then I saw her again. It said "Rita Hayworth," but I would have recognized her anyway. She was on the cover of *Modern Screen* and it was in color and . . . she had red hair! It was like a sign.

I had red hair, too. Auburn, just like hers. My mother liked to call it something else, brown with red highlights, but that wasn't true. I knew why she said that, though. In Vienna, red hair meant Jewish, and then when Hitler came, it was the worst color hair to have. My mother and sister, Hedi, could still have gone to the park in Vienna where we used to play, even though all those new signs went up, but it would have been too risky to take me. But on 191st Street and Wadsworth Avenue in New York City, where almost everyone was Irish, red hair was okay. Sometimes grown-ups would smile at me as they passed and say, "Oh, another cute little colleen," and I'd feel all warm from their approval.

Well, I had to have that magazine, so I ran the rest of the way home.

"Mother, can I have fifteen cents?"

I called them "Mother" and "Father" and it sounds unfriendly, but it wasn't that at all. They used to be "Mutti" and "Vatti," but I wasn't talking German anymore. When you give up a language, you give up all your baby words and you can't just adopt those words in a new language. "Mommy," "Daddy," "peepee." It was too late for that. And "Mom" and "Dad" sounded unnatural coming from me.

"Mother, please, can I have fifteen cents?"

"Fifteen cents?"

"There's a magazine all about Rita Hayworth and I

have to find out all about her and it's at Jackandandy's and please, I want to buy it right now and—"

"Liesl, not so fast! Catch your breath—"

"But I want to buy it right now and I have to know who she is and—"

"All right, all right, wait a minute."

She was ironing the covers for the down quilts, the white ones with the blue forget-me-not embroidery around the monogram. The steam from the iron had dampened her forehead, and she wiped it with the back of her hand and pushed her upsweep back into place.

"Please . . ."

She hesitated and then carefully fished some coins out of the brown leather pocketbook. She always hesitated before she counted out money, and I knew I couldn't always call up to the window for a nickel for candy, the way some of the kids did. We had a lot of nice things from before—thin, thin china dishes with delicate violet flowers that you could see right through and red-and-blue Persian rugs with a thousand curlicues to trace with my toes—but we didn't have enough dimes and nickels and quarters.

"All right," she said, "and go to the—"

"Thank you, Mother!"

"—go to the bakery. Say 'sour rye sliced for twelve.' Now remember, sliced. And I want the *small* size."

"Okay," I called, half out the door, "sour rye sliced for twelve!"

I ran all the way there and all the way back. I slid the bread onto the kitchen counter and I dove into the magazine. My sister looked over my shoulder.

"Dumbhead!" Hedi said. "It's only a movie magazine. Rita Hayworth is only on the cover."

"I knew that," I said. I hadn't. I was disappointed that the pages were filled with all kinds of other things.

"Look at this," Hedi said. "You can't even understand this."

"I can too!"

"Mother, she can't even read this! She's too little, she can't even understand this!"

"I can too!" I hated Hedi when she acted older just because she was.

"All right, what does this mean? 'The gobs vote Betty Grable the gal with the number-one gams.' You understand that? 'Are Lana Turner and Turhan Bey on the rocks?' You understand that?"

Well, it wasn't the way we had been taught in English lessons back in Vienna, with the British lady. Then there were words like "frock" and "pram" and boys named Christopher Robin. But I kept getting magazines with wonderful names like *Silver Screen* and it didn't take too long to learn American slang and get into an exciting new world.

There was Veronica Lake with the peekaboo hair and pinup girls and all the big studios like Columbia and Paramount and Warner Bros. and, the best of all,

Metro-Goldwyn-Mayer in Culver City, California. And Lana Turner was just a high school girl in a sweater drinking soda through a straw at Schwab's Drugstore and she was discovered right there by a talent scout. There were a lot of very useful things, too, like the secrets of glamour and the multiple-choice quiz that taught you how to handle different problems. Like, What do you do when a soldier calls you unexpectedly and he only has an eight-hour pass and your hair is dirty and you were going to wash it that night? "(a) Tell him you can't go out because you have to wash your hair" is wrong, of course, because that's bad for his morale and would hurt the war effort. "(b) Go out with your dirty hair hanging there" is wrong because he'll surely notice it and never call you again. "(c) Put your hair in an upsweep with a flower on the side and greet him with a big smile" is right because grease doesn't show as much in upswept hair and the flower and your dazzling smile will distract him. I was really glad to be learning about things like that and the true meaning of "oomph." Ann Sheridan was the "Oomph Girl," but Rita Hayworth would always, always be my favorite and I was going to be a movie star.

"You can't be a movie star," Hedi said once.

"Why?"

"Because movie stars can't have freckles."

"Oh, go soak your head!"

I didn't care because I was prettier than Hedi any-

7

way, even if she was older, and I knew I'd be discovered someday, and just to help it along, I sometimes sang on the way to school. "Don't Sit Under the Apple Tree" was my best song. I sang loudest when I got to the corner of St. Nicholas Avenue and 191st Street, where it was busy, just in case some M-G-M talent scouts were lurking in the subway arcade.

I didn't believe in talent scouts all that much, not deep in my heart, but you never knew, and a play was a play, after all, even at P.S. 189. When Mrs. Hallandale said that the fifth grade would do a Christmas play for the whole school, I knew just how *Modern Screen* would describe it years and years from now. "It was only a schoolgirl who stepped out on the humble stage of P.S. 189, but on that wintry afternoon, a star was born. . . ."

We had to wait a whole week for Mrs. Hallandale to finish writing the script and give out the parts. For that whole week I tried my hardest to sit still with my hands folded on my desk and do other dumb, good things. And then, all in one morning, Mrs. Hallandale gave me a speaking part and went ahead and ruined the very first rehearsal!

Mrs. Hallandale, with her narrow pursed lips and her squinchy pale eyes, didn't know anything! I was walking home from school feeling rotten and I should have been running and happy and coming into the apartment all out of breath, calling, "I got a part! I got a part!" Actually, the best part went to Alice. The play was called *Christmas in Many Lands*, and Alice was going to be the American girl and come into all the scenes. I knew Mrs. Hallandale would never give me anything as good as that. Alice looked like one of the Campbell Soup Kids and she had everything I wanted: Mary Janes instead of oxfords, knees that were never scraped or scabby, and a mother who was a PTA lady and sent important messages to the teachers.

The scene I did get, though, could be terrific. I was going to be the French girl, a teenager at least, and Edward was going to be the American soldier and we'd say lines about how sad Christmas was in France this year with the war and everything, but I had a Noël log anyway and we hoped there'd be peace soon. I liked it a lot because, even though it wasn't in the scene the dumb way Mrs. Hallandale wrote it, I thought the French girl and the American soldier would fall in love and then he'd have to go off to war and she'd cry and run after the train and she'd have a brother like Jean-Pierre Aumont in the Underground. So even though my scene was only a few lines, I could imagine the rest and be Madeleine Carroll, ladylike but sexy, in that nice French way. It would be like the beginning of a Warner Bros. movie.

We went down to the auditorium for rehearsal. I was awfully glad I wasn't in the Mexican part, because all they did was break the piñata and yell "Feliz Navidad" at the end. I was happy about my part, and then Mrs. Hallandale spoiled everything. I had started saying the lines to Edward, just the way Madeleine Carroll would, but Mrs. Hallandale stopped me and told me to face front. I thought she meant just a little more, so I turned my body a little. Then she stopped me again and went up on the stage and turned me roughly, the whole way.

"But Mrs. Hallandale," I said, "I'm supposed to be talking to Edward."

"Never mind about that. You just face front."

"But Mrs. Hallandale, it's not natural to—"

"I want the audience to hear every single word. Why do you always have to talk back and be a troublemaker?"

"If I turn just a little bit toward Edward, they could still hear—"

"If you can't do as you're told, I'll give someone else the part."

She would have, too. So I did it the way she said. We all had to go to the very front of the stage for our lines and stare straight out at the audience. I couldn't even see Edward when I said, "Welcome to Free France!" It was so dumb and I'd make a fool of myself, and if, just if, by any chance, a talent scout just happened to be there, he wouldn't discover me.

And then, to make everything worse, my so-called friend Teresa said, "The only reason she gave you the French girl was because you have an accent." That was a filthy lie, because I didn't anymore and Teresa was just jealous because she was only in the Swedish crowd scene holding the glögg.

I was stomping home, thinking about Mrs. Hallandale and how much I hated her. For one thing, she did everything in size places and I was one of the tall girls and I was tired of sitting in the back of the room and being last for everything. She called me "Lie-sell" all year, rhyming with "high sell," "Lie-sell Rosen," and my name is Liesl, rhyming with "measle." I wished I could think of a better word to rhyme it with, but it didn't matter, because when I was a movie star, I'd change my name anyway, to Flame Flynn. Greer Garson, Maria Montez, Flame Flynn. And when they interviewed me for *Modern Screen,* I'd say—and I didn't care who read it—I'd say, "My fifth grade teacher at P.S. 189, Mrs. Hallandale, almost destroyed my career because she didn't know anything about plays or acting or anything. But fortunately, I knew even then, even in Mrs. Hallandale's dumb play, how to—"

"Hey, jerk, you're talking to yourself."

Billy Laramie was leaning against the red brick of the building. He was smoking, right where everyone could see him, right under his own window, the one with the blue star for his father away in the war. He was one of the big boys, and I must have really been saying stuff out loud for him to notice me and be laughing.

"I am not talking to myself! I'm in a play and I'm practicing my lines." I could feel myself starting to blush and I hated myself for it. Rita Hayworth would

11

never have blushed.

"Oh yeah?"

"But Mrs. Hallandale is making me do it all wrong" came bursting out, "and she called me a troublemaker!"

He was grinning. "Well, that's nothin'. They call me that all the time."

"What grade are you in?" I said.

"Seventh."

"I'm in fifth."

"How come Old Lady Hallandale called you a troublemaker?"

"She hates me, that's all. I was the only girl in the whole class that got a B in conduct." I said it like it was nothing, but it had really hurt to be singled out like that.

"I thought you'd be good in school, like your sister. She's a stuck-up bookworm."

"Are you in my sister's class?"

"Yeah."

"She's not stuck-up. She's smart and she just likes to read a lot." I liked to read, too, but I didn't want anyone calling me a bookworm.

"Well, I'm smart," he said. "Street smart, not in school."

"I bet you could be if you wanted to," I said. "In school, I mean."

"Yeah, I know," he said, "but I don't like them tellin' me what to do all the time."

"I know. I don't either."

He took a long drag on the cigarette and let the smoke out slowly in a blue-gray stream. He left the cigarette dangling from his lips, like Alan Ladd in *This Gun for Hire*.

"Aren't you scared your mother'll see you smoking?"

"Not my mother, my father's wife." He had a way of tilting his head a little to the side, with his chin up. "She can't tell me nothin'."

Down the street some kids were playing stickball, and we watched them changing sides after the third out.

"Wait till my dad gets home from the war," he said. "He'll straighten her out all right."

I wondered about the mean way he talked about Mrs. Laramie. I liked her. She was young and pretty, with long, jet-black hair and bright-red lipstick and sparkly earrings. She was always standing around in front of the building with Billy's little sister and talking to someone and laughing. She smiled and said hello whenever I passed by.

"Why don't you like her?" I said.

He turned and looked at me. I'd seen Billy around on the street and he had no-color brown hair and wore faded, dingy clothes. I'd never noticed before how deep blue his eyes were, the bluest blue I had ever seen, and how fierce. I shouldn't have asked.

He almost scared me and then his face relaxed. "You

really don't know, do you?"

"No," I said.

He turned back to the stickball game. "Look at O'Donnell. He catches like a girl."

"I guess so."

"So what's old Hallandale doin' to you?"

I told him the whole thing about facing front.

"Yeah, that's dumb all right." Another drag and he aimed the butt in a long arc into the gutter. "Okay, here's what you do. You just keep on goin' the way she says. Once the show is on, though, you're the boss, see? You go and do whatever you want. How's she gonna stop you? She can't go runnin' up on the stage."

I thought about it and I nodded.

He was laughing. "Boy, old Hallandale's gonna pee in her pants! Hey, you gonna have the guts?"

The way he was laughing made me laugh, too. "I will. You watch me!"

"Okay, Rosen! All right!" He had a good smile.

When I went into the house, he called after me, "Hey! Don't let 'em get you down!"

I thought Billy Laramie was nice. Even if he used bad words and smoked and acted tough like everyone said, I thought he was most especially nice.

2

Hedi and I were listening to Burns and Allen on the radio when the air raid sirens sounded. For a blackout, I liked *Inner Sanctum* best. Once we listened to it in the dark, and the creaking door they had in the beginning was perfect. I loved spooky things. Burns and Allen were good, too, because of all the dumb, funny things Gracie said.

Hedi raced me to the living room window to pull down the blackout shade, and she got there first, so I turned off the ceiling light.

"Always when I am studying," Father said. He put down the medical textbook and stretched. Mother came in from the kitchen carrying a dish towel. With only the little utility light on, her body threw long shadows.

Hedi and I opened the side of the shade a crack and

watched the lights go out one by one in the buildings across the street. There was a light left on the fifth floor for the longest time and then finally it went out, too.

I thought air raids were fun because something always happened. Mr. Sullivan, our air raid warden, strutted down the street looking important and always wound up arguing with somebody. In Vienna, it was different. When the sirens sounded there, it was serious and sad and quiet. I could remember saying, "Are the bad men coming to bomb us?" and Father answering, "If anyone bombs us, they're the good people." I was too little to understand it then, though he tried and tried to explain. I took the idea of being bombed personally. No real bombs came there, either, but it was different. In America, we could be on the same side as everyone else, and that felt good.

"Look," Hedi said, "someone has a light on."

We could see light coming from our building, but we couldn't tell whose window. We waited to see what Mr. Sullivan would do.

"Hey, you there, you on the third floor!" Loud and raspy. "Turn it off!"

Nothing happened. We could still see the light's reflection on the sidewalk.

"Hey, you, whaddya think you're doing? Sendin' a secret message to Tojo?"

"Aw, Frank, give me just a minute, won't you?" The silky voice was Mrs. Laramie's. I never knew Mr. Sullivan's first name was Frank.

"Oh, it's you, Kate, is it?" He altogether stopped snarling and his voice turned soft. "Well, you see, you got to get that light turned off."

"One second, Frank. I only have two little nails to go."

"My God!" Hedi was giggling. "She's polishing her nails in a blackout!"

Father laughed behind me. "Americans have no discipline."

"But you like Americans, don't you?" I asked. I wanted us all to be Americans. I wanted to be the Average American Girl.

"Yes," Father said. "Yes, I do. Sometimes not too much discipline is a good thing." His face had turned serious.

I watched out the window and waited for Mr. Sullivan to yell and carry on. This time, Mr. Sullivan only sounded embarrassed.

"Come on now, Katie," he said, "there's a war on."

"Dammit! I'm turning the goddamn light off!" That was Billy's voice, and the hoarse way he sounded made me feel bad. "Okay, show's over! Keep movin', Sullivan!"

We watched the sidewalk turn dark.

"That Mrs. Laramie." Mother shook her head. "Even with Mr. Sullivan."

"What?"

No one answered me.

"What about Mrs. Laramie and Mr. Sullivan?" I knew the women in the neighborhood talked about her.

"Nothing," Mother said. "It is the way she talks and behaves."

"I like her," I said. "I think she's so pretty and friendly."

"Very, very friendly," Hedi said. "Very extremely friendly."

"Hedi, stop that," Father said. "People gossip too much."

"But Father, everyone knows . . ." Hedi said.

"That's enough. There are worse things in the world that people do."

I thought I'd better not ask, because Father looked so stern. I was pretty sure they meant that Mrs. Laramie was a loose woman. That sounded exciting and glamorous. The more I thought about it, the more I could see that she was almost a Linda Darnell type. Sultry and Seductive. I liked Mrs. Laramie more than ever, but then I remembered the other part of it. Mr. Laramie was away in the service and that made her the wrong kind of woman, the kind who wrote "Dear John" letters, the second lead who would have a bad end.

I wondered if that was why the Laramies didn't go to church on Sundays.

On Sunday mornings, a hush settled over the street and the boys wore suits and ties and the girls wore hats and red Sunday coats. Even after church, they would stand around stiffly, afraid to spoil their good clothes, hardly moving. I didn't like Sunday mornings. I didn't like the quiet on the street without handball, stickball, double Dutch, roller hockey, ring-a-levio. And once a little girl walked by holding her mother's hand and stared at me and said, "Look! She isn't wearing a hat!"

Sometimes I'd see Billy Laramie standing on the corner talking with the big boys, and he looked out of place, too, in everyday faded clothes. I was pretty sure he was Catholic, and I wondered about him.

One Sunday morning there was no one on the street except Billy and me.

I was bouncing a Spalding against the red brick wall, practicing hard slams for Chinese handball, and whenever it hit the edge of a brick, it careened off in some crazy direction. I was getting tired of chasing it. Billy was a few yards away, leaning against the wall, looking bored. I chased the ball for the last time and caught up to it right near Billy and said, "Hi."

"Hi."

"There's no one to play with," I said. "I guess everyone's in church."

"Yeah."

"There's nothing to do," I said.

He shrugged.

I wanted to ask why he didn't go to church, but I didn't dare.

"Where's your little sister?" I said. Mary was only three and she was fun to play with sometimes, like playing dolls.

"Inside with Kate."

"She's so cute," I said.

"Well, this stinks." He stood up straight. "I'm gonna go on an adventure."

"Where? Can I come?"

He considered for a minute. "No, you better not."

"Why? Where are you going?"

"You'd be scared."

"No I wouldn't. What are you going to do?"

"I'm gonna go ride the trolley on Broadway. Maybe go on up to Fort Tryon."

I thought, What was so scary about riding a trolley? And then I realized what he meant. He was talking about hanging on at the back.

"See you later," he said.

"Wait. I'll go with you." I'd seen kids hanging on the backs of trolleys when I was with Mother. Mother called them "street children" and she said they sometimes fell off and got run over, or couldn't get off fast enough when two trolleys moved together, and got crushed.

"Up to you," he said. "If you chicken out, you walk back by yourself, okay?"

"Okay." I wondered if you could get electrocuted from one of those wires. I tried to remember what Mother had said.

There were two ways down to Broadway. One was through Wadsworth Terrace, going down and down long, steep flights of stairs. The short way was the subway tunnel. We went down the subway elevator with its creaky iron gate and passed by the turnstiles and went into the tunnel.

It was at least a block long and barely lit. My eyes had to get used to it. The walls were damp.

"My sister, Hedi, says there are bats in here."

"Maybe."

"I don't think so, though, do you?"

"Maybe. Bats like caves."

"Well, this isn't a cave. This is a tunnel."

"Dracula!" Billy yelled. "Drac-U-LA!" The sound came back.

"Hello!" I called and I heard a faint "hello."

"Echo!" I called. "Echo!"

"Billy Laramie! Billy Terence Laramie!" His words came back garbled. "It don't work so good with something long."

"Liesl!" I called.

"Billy!"

It came back. Liesl, Billy. Liesl, Billy. Liesl, Billy.

An old man going in the opposite direction passed us and gave us a dirty look.

Then we were running and laughing and our footsteps made echoes of their own.

We blinked in the pale winter sunshine when we came out on Broadway.

"Okay," he said. "Do what I do. You wait until they're just about to move or else the conductor'll catch you. Jump up and grab on quick with both hands."

I was still carrying the Spalding. "What should I do with it?"

"Stick it in your pocket, dope."

"It won't fit."

"Give it to me." He stuck it inside his shirt.

A trolley came to the stop on the uptown side and Billy moved to the back of it. I followed him. Passengers were getting off and three people were waiting to get on. My heart was beating. We watched the people getting on. The last was a slow, fat lady with brown grocery bags.

"Now!"

Billy jumped up on the back and then I was right next to him, hanging on. My heart was going fast and I held on so tight, the metal bars were cutting into my hands. I felt us starting to move.

Billy was grinning at me. "I didn't think you were gonna do it."

I could see the electric connection up on top. I wondered if it was like a third rail. We were picking up speed and there were cars behind us and all around us and I could see the metal tracks underneath.

"Hey, take it easy and enjoy it!"

I looked at Billy, and his hair was blowing and he had a big smile. I could feel the wind, my hair blowing behind me, and more gusts of wind on my legs, puffing out my dress and my coat. It was almost like sledding standing up. I stopped hanging on so tight. I knew I wasn't going to fall off.

"Duck your head to the side so they can't see you," he said.

The trolley shook to a stop and more passengers got off and then it started again. I liked it when it picked up speed. And there wasn't any other trolley around to get too close and crush me.

"Fun, huh?"

I nodded hard.

Mother and Father would be so upset if they could see me. I could almost hear the way Mother said "street children." What she meant was children with dirty faces who no one took good care of or taught good manners. Not like Hedi and me.

But it was fun!

A car right behind us honked and honked.

"Go blow it out your nose!" Billy yelled, laughing.

Billy was fresh, but funny.

"Next stop's the last one. Jump off on the sidewalk side," he said.

Then I was standing on the sidewalk with shaky legs. We were standing right across from the entrance to Fort Tryon Park.

"Hey! You're all right!" Billy said, and I felt good.

We went up to the top of Fort Tryon Park. There was a lookout point where you could see the Hudson

River and the Palisades. It was getting cold, and the river and the rocks and the sky were steel gray.

"I used to live over there," Billy said.

"The Palisades?"

"New Jersey, but the other part. You can't see it from here. That was before."

"Before what?"

"Just before. You ever been to the Cloisters?"

"No."

"Come on. It's good. They got armor."

We went through a courtyard with arches and no one was there but us. There was a water fountain and I started to get a drink.

"Hey, don't! That's holy water!"

"Oh," I said. Something about the place made me whisper. "Billy, what is this?" I whispered.

"Some kind of museum."

Inside, it was very quiet and too dark to get a good look at the hangings on the wall. There was one with a goat with one horn and a fence all around. There were lots of things with crosses.

"Billy, is this some kind of church?"

"No."

"Is it something religious?"

"Yeah."

Billy found the armor and looked at it for a long time.

"Ain't that something!"

"It's okay." I was getting bored.

"Look at that!" He walked around and looked at every single piece.

"Come on, let's go," I said.

"Wait a minute. . . . Hey, look at this one over here. Boy, nobody could get to you in that thing!"

Finally we went back outside. It was cold and there was something heavy hanging in the air, like it wanted to snow soon. The cold was making my lips feel chapped.

"Is that really holy water?"

"Could be."

"Are you Catholic?"

"Yeah."

I thought I knew him well enough to ask now, after hanging on to the trolley and everything. "How come you don't go to church on Sundays?"

"Because of my mother."

"You mean Mrs. Laramie doesn't want you to?"

"No, not Kate. Because of my real mother."

He was quiet for such a long time that I didn't think he'd say anything else. He was moving pebbles around with his toe.

"My mother killed herself and they wouldn't bury her in the regular Catholic cemetery on account of it's a sin, so my dad got mad and stopped going to church and I stopped, too." He said it without any expression, the words running together, looking down at the pebbles.

I just stood there, thinking why and how, and thinking that Billy was different from all the other kids on the block, too.

He looked at me and his eyes were mean and blazing blue. "You wanted to know so bad. Well, now you know."

He walked away from me, over to a low stone wall, and looked out in the direction of the Hudson. His head was tilted to the side a little, chin up, in that certain way he had.

"I'm sorry," I said.

"Yeah, yeah," without turning around.

I stayed where I was and watched his back. I was sorry about both: about his mother and about asking. I hoped he understood that.

When he finally turned around, he was acting regular again and said, "You forgot something."

He pulled the Spalding out of his shirt and threw it to me. I caught it and was surprised to find the warmth from his body on it.

3

I hoped Hedi wouldn't have to go to the bathroom and bother me, because I was practicing being Rita Hayworth in the bathroom mirror and it took a long time. I was working on the smile. The whole trick to it was showing both your upper and lower teeth and keeping them parted.

I could hear the radio from the living room. It was Gabriel Heatter and he was saying, "Ah, there's good news tonight." It didn't make sense, because he always said that even if there was bad news from England and France and Russia. Hedi listened to the news with Father and talked to him about the battle of Stalingrad and sometimes she took the war maps from *The New York Times* and drew on them with black pencil the way she thought the armies should go next. She was always surrounding the Germans with pincer attacks, and Father listened to her very seriously. I wished that I had something to talk to him about that was as interesting to him. He didn't care anything about movie stars. Anyway, the news was on and I could hear Hedi and Father talking in there, so Hedi wouldn't be interrupting me for a while.

When I threw my head back, the smile looked just right. It would have been perfect with long hair. My hair only came down to my chin. Next time Mother wanted to take me to the barber, I'd put up a real fight.

My cheeks ached from smiling and I thought I'd practice crying. I wanted to do it like Margaret O'Brien in *Journey for Margaret,* with her face all still and nice and just one fat tear running down her cheek. Teresa said that the way they do it in Hollywood is they put things in their eyes, like pepper, and that makes their eyes tear. I never knew whether to believe Teresa or not. She was always telling stories like that. Teresa said that Rita Hayworth's real name was Margarita Cansino and she had black hair and dyed it red and—and here's the worst part—that her forehead was too low and they did electrolysis to get rid of all the hair and raise it. I called her a liar and we got into a big fight about it.

I couldn't get one nice fat tear to run down. It would be different if I were in a movie. I knew I could do it in a movie. In movies, people cried at the right times and laughed at the right times. It worked out the way it was supposed to.

Real life was messy and you never knew what anyone would do. Even Mother and Father. Mother
hardly ever cried, and then, when she did, it was over
things I'd never have expected.

There was the night she went to the PTA meeting.
When she came home again, Hedi and I were playing
Chinese checkers and eating walnuts and Father was
studying his medical textbook. She came in and
slammed the door behind her and, as soon as the door
was shut, she exploded into tears, as if she'd been
holding it back all the way home.

Father jumped up from the couch. "What is it?
What happened, Franya?"

She was crying. "I didn't understand one word.
They talked so fast. I could not understand. . . ."

"It's all right."

"No, it's not." She kept stopping and swallowing.
"How can I bring up my daughters? How can I be a
mother to them if I can't go to the school? If I don't
know what is going on?"

"Franya . . ."

"I sat there like an idiot. I couldn't understand one
word of one speech."

Father had his arm around her. "Hedi and Liesl will
be fine. It does not matter." He looked over at us and
his look was ordering us to be fine.

She was crying with loud gulps.

He led her into their bedroom and said, over his
shoulder, "Get ready for bed, girls. Immediately." It

was too early, but when Father said things in that way, we didn't argue.

Just before he closed their door, I heard him say, "You do not have to go to meetings. They are intelligent girls, they will do well and . . ." and their voices became low. I could hear them talking quietly for a long time into the night.

"What happened?" I whispered to Hedi.

"Nothing," Hedi whispered back. "It was because the ladies were talking English so fast."

The other time was right after they went to the movies. They went to see *The Grapes of Wrath* because it was by John Steinbeck and he was famous in Vienna, too. That time it wasn't real crying. Her eyes were watery and she was biting her lips and she was standing, hugging herself as if she were cold. The worst part was the drawn look on Father's face.

"They were native-born Americans," he said. "They knew the language, they—"

"I know you will pass the test and you will get a license." Mother's words were good, but she sounded shaky.

Father sighed.

"It is only a matter of time," Mother said. "You will be a doctor again."

"Time? How long can we hold out? How much longer? We are strangers. We are not familiar with the customs here. And if native-born Americans couldn't—"

"It was in the Depression, Manek. The Depression is over."

"But Hans Bloch failed the test! How could that be? Hans Bloch is a brilliant diagnostician and yet he . . ." Father's voice trailed off as he took off his coat.

Mother went into the kitchen and started to do things at the stove. I was hungry and dinner was late. Father sat at the dining table and stared into its dark-brown top. I was always proud of how big and well muscled he was, but now even his body looked defeated. Was it something in the movie? Was it because Dr. Bloch had failed the medical boards? But we had heard about that days ago. Father and some of the other men had gone to his home in Brooklyn to encourage him.

"What was the movie about?" I asked.

"It was about the Okies," Father said. "People from Oklahoma. They lost their farms and they went to California to pick fruit."

"They were starving," Mother said. She was setting the table and her eyes still had that watery look. "I didn't know conditions were so bad."

When we ate dinner, the room was very quiet, except for the scrape of knives against plates and the ticking of the porcelain clock on the secretary. I concentrated on chewing and swallowing each mouthful of meat. Hedi looked pale and she didn't say anything. No one was talking at all, and I pushed the meat around on my plate because it was hard to swallow.

Suddenly Father gave a short laugh and I looked up, startled.

"Look at us!" he said. "We are eating your mother's wonderful wiener schnitzel and we worry about starving! A foolish loss of courage, and all from one of Liesl's Metro-Goldwyn-Mayer movies. Next time we go to see Charlie Chaplin!"

Father made everything all right again and my appetite came back. We were having wiener schnitzel with anchovies, and cucumber salad, and that was my favorite meal in the whole world, even though in my heart I wished we ate American food like Campbell's vegetable soup and hamburgers and Tip-Top cupcakes. . . .

"Is there any money left from the bracelet?" Hedi asked. Her face still looked pinched.

"Yes," Mother said. "Hedi, you are too big a worrier for such a young girl."

"What? What bracelet?" I looked from Mother to Hedi. "What do you mean, money from the bracelet?" Hedi always knew about things that they forgot to tell me!

"We were allowed to take only thirty-two dollars out of Austria," Father said, "but do you know what your mother did?"

"What?"

"We were allowed to send our household goods ahead to America," Mother said. "We had some gold Maria Theresa coins—they were a present from a patient—and my diamond-and-gold bracelet, and our wedding rings, of course, and . . . Well, on the day of the decree that Jews could no longer own gold, I opened up our mattresses and tucked things into the middle and sewed them in. And when we arrived in America, they were here, waiting for us."

"Did you really do that?" I said. Mother looked delicate and fragile. I would never think of her doing something dangerous.

"Thirty-two dollars to start again in a strange country!" Father said. "May Hitler turn into a light bulb, to hang all day and burn all night!"

"But what if the Nazis had found everything? Weren't you afraid?"

"I didn't think anyone would search feather mattresses and down pillows. Can you imagine the mess that would be? Down flying all over and into their noses and making them sneeze!" Mother was trying hard to be funny; she wasn't as good at it as Father, but Hedi smiled a little. "And we still have money left from the bracelet."

"But what about Dr. Bloch?" I said. "Why did he fail the test?"

Father took a deep breath. "I don't know. There must be an explanation. Some logical explanation."

"Maybe he was too nervous," Mother said. "Maybe his English was not good enough."

"His English is better than mine," Father said sharply.

"But he will try again, nevertheless," Mother said. "He cannot give up."

Father nodded and reached for her hand. They held hands on the table, between the saltshaker and the butter dish.

"Girls, the important thing to remember is that nobody can take away what you have in your head." Father was looking at me and Hedi, but I thought he was talking to himself as much as to us. "Please remember this, always. Knowledge is the only lasting security. No one can ever take that away from you."

Hedi nodded. I loved the way he looked now, strong and serious, so I nodded, too, just to please him. He didn't know that, when I was a movie star, my face would be my fortune and nothing bad could happen then.

4

I liked Grace Flanagan right away. Usually, when someone was new in school, they'd act shy or at least wait until someone talked to them first, and it took a while until they fit in. Not Grace. When she was new, she came up to me with a big smile and said, "Hi! My name's Grace Flanagan. What's yours?" I liked her right away.

I never saw her after school because she lived all the way over on Amsterdam Avenue, but one day she and Teresa and I were talking near the coat closet about what we'd be when we grew up and I decided I liked her a lot better than Teresa.

"I want to be a movie star," I said, "and my name will be Flame Flynn."

"You're always saying that," Teresa said.

"Because that's what I'm going to be."

"I mean for real," Teresa said. "I'm going to be a secretary. I'm going to secretarial school and everything. I'm going to work in an office."

"I want to be a singer," Grace said, "like Alice Faye."

Teresa made her superior face. "My mother says being a secretary is practical and they make real good money, too."

"So can singers," said Grace.

"I'm talking about for real," Teresa said.

"So am I," Grace said. "I can get money for singing. I need more Christmas money and I'm going to sing for it."

"Yeah, sure," Teresa said.

Grace didn't even mind the sour look on Teresa's face. "I bet I need more Christmas money than anybody," she continued. "I've got three sisters and two brothers, and my oldest brother, Tim, is in the Air Force, so I want to get him something extra nice, and then there's—"

Mrs. Hallandale shushed us and gave me a dirty look. I wasn't even the one doing the talking! We all had to line up in size places and wait to be dismissed. I wanted to talk to Grace some more, but she was in the middle part of the line. She was going to be a movie star, too! A singer like Alice Faye. She sounded serious about it. I always thought I'd be a dancer like Rita Hayworth. The only problem was that you had to have lessons for dancing, and we couldn't afford any kind of lessons. But singing? All you had to do was open your mouth and sing, you didn't need any kind of lessons! I wondered if Grace would mind if I was a singing movie star, too.

Finally Mrs. Hallandale said, "Class dismissed!" and I caught up to Grace.

"You thought of it first," I said, "so if you mind, I won't be a singing movie star."

"That's okay," Grace said. "I don't mind."

"You're sure?" I knew Teresa would have made a big fuss about having thought of it first and all that.

"It's okay, honest. You could be like . . . Judy Garland?"

"Thanks, Grace. No, not Judy. Rita Hayworth. She sings sometimes. She did in *You Were Never Lovelier*. In *My Gal Sal*, too."

"I heard they put someone else's voice in for her," Grace said, "but that doesn't matter, you could be a singing Rita Hayworth. You look something like her, too, your coloring and everything. I love Alice Faye, though, don't you? I love the way she sings." Grace started to sing some of the lines from "When the Lights Go On Again," and she really did sound good. In assembly you could always hear Grace's voice loud and clear over everyone else's.

"Grace, what did you mean before, about singing for Christmas money?"

"Well, you just go and sing, and if people like the way you sound, they give you money."

"What do you mean? Where?"

"Anywhere. In the backyards. Do you want to go with me this afternoon?"

"Sure. I don't really know how, though."

"It's easy," Grace said. "Let's go home and get washed up first. We gotta look nice. I'll meet you over at the candy store and we'll get a song sheet."

Grace was waiting for me in front of the candy store, reading the song sheet.

"This is a good one," she said. "It has 'Don't Get Around Much Anymore' and 'G.I. Jive' and 'Coming In on a Wing and a Prayer.' "

"I try to memorize the lyrics from the radio."

"It's hard to get all the lyrics that way. Look, I paid a dime for this, so the first nickel we get goes to me and we split the rest half and half, okay?"

"Okay. What do we do now?"

"Let's go someplace and rehearse."

We went into the nearest building, because it was so cold out, and we sat down on the stairs above the mailboxes. Grace took a lipstick out of her pocket. It was Pond's Pink Dither.

"I stole it from my sister Peggy. I'll sneak it back before she even misses it. We have to wear makeup, though, don't you think?"

"We have to look nice," I said. I still wasn't sure how this was going to work, so I thought I'd just follow Grace.

"I can get it on straight without even looking."

Grace looked different and older with her lips bright pink. "Do you want me to do yours?"

"Okay."

"I'd better not squash the point, because Peggy'll kill me." It felt funny to have something put on my lips. "That looks super-duper, Liesl!"

"Call me Flame."

"Okay, Flame. You think I oughtta change my name, too? Grace Flanagan doesn't sound right, does it? I can't think of anything else, though."

"I'll think up something for you," I said. "I'm good at that."

"Okay," she said. "Now pinch your cheeks until they hurt. That way they get all nice and rosy. If people like the way you look, they throw you more money."

"Throw it?"

"Sure, from their windows. Let's get started. We'll sing everything through once, but not too loud or else we'll get chased out of here. When we really do it, you sing as loud as you can, so they hear you all the way up to the fifth floor. You know how to harmonize?"

"No, I'm sorry."

"Oh, that's all right. Let's do "Don't Get Around Much Anymore" first. It was number one on *The Hit Parade* last week."

"I know. It's my favorite program."

"Me too. I even like it when they go 'LSMFT! LSMFT! Lucky Strike Means Fine Tobacco!' But what do they mean when they say 'Lucky Strike Green Has Gone to War'? I don't get that."

"I don't either," I said. Billy Laramie smoked Lucky Strikes. I'd ask him—he'd know. I felt like saying something about Billy Laramie to Grace, but then I didn't want to sound like I was showing off about being friends with him.

We sang the songs and I just sang along softly, listening to Grace. She sounded really good, holding some notes for a long time and snapping her fingers with "G.I. Jive" and everything.

"Okay, we're ready," she said. "Remember to smile all the time. Everyone likes you when you smile."

I followed Grace out to the sidewalk and then down through a cellar entrance.

"Have you ever done this before?" I said.

"Sure. Lots of times."

We passed some metal garbage cans and then we were in the alley between three buildings. There were some wash lines high up, with sheets flapping in the wind.

"This is a good one," Grace said.

"Why?"

"Because you get three buildings all at once. Usually it's just two."

Grace started to sing "Don't Get Around Much Anymore" loud and clear. She was smiling hard and her dimples stood out and her eyes were shining. I sang along with her and thought of what a pretty, open face she had.

When we finished, she muttered under her breath, "Smile, Flame."

Something came falling down, ringing against the pavement. And then more.

"Curtsy!" she muttered, smiling hard. I curtsied and tried to do it the way Grace did. She swept down low, with her head up, smiling hard and raising her arm, like she was waving at a window way up high. Then she stood up and started "G.I. Jive" and I followed her.

Again, the ring of a few coins, her deep curtsy and smile, and both arms raised high over her head. She didn't even look like herself. She was somebody magical, glittering on a real stage. And then she was just another kid again and we were picking up pennies and nickels and a few dimes.

Her face was radiant. "Two songs at a time is enough," she said, laughing. "More than that and they might dump water on us. You never know."

She led me to another building and another and another. We kept changing songs so we wouldn't get bored. We put in "Deep in the Heart of Texas" after "Comin' In on a Wing and a Prayer" and there were more pennies and nickels. I was freezing. My fingers were hurting from the cold, and I wished I had brought mittens. Grace said not to sing with my hands in my coat pockets because it didn't look right.

"Come on, one more," Grace said. We were on

188th Street. "I've got hardly anything saved up."

"I'm freezing," I said.

"One more. I want to get something good for my brother Tim."

"Not this building," I said. "The super's a drunk and he stays in the cellar and he hates kids."

"That doesn't bother me." She was smiling brilliantly, dimples flashing. "Nothing bothers me. Are you afraid to go down that cellar?"

"Kind of."

"All right, we'll go one building over."

"Grace, I'm freezing. Let's quit now."

"Yeah, me too. Let's count up."

We had three dollars and sixty-five cents. That was one dollar and eighty cents each, with the extra nickel going to Grace for the song sheet.

"I never made any money before," I said.

"I have, lots of times. Sometimes my sister Maureen goes with me. Doesn't it make you feel like you're in show business?"

"How about Candy Cornell? For your stage name."

"Oh, that's nice! Candy Cornell. That's really nice!"

"You can have it."

"Thanks. See you tomorrow, Flame."

"So long, Candy."

It was dark when I came home.

"Where have you been?" Mother was grating carrots into the salad bowl. "Wash up for supper. What is that on your lips?"

"Pink Dither. I've been working," I said, "in show business."

"What?"

"And look! One dollar and eighty cents!" I handed it to her proudly.

"What? Where did you get this?"

"I was singing with my friend and people liked us and—"

"Oh, God! Where?"

"In the backyards, and Grace says sometimes you can make a lot more, but I got too cold and—"

"In backyards! Oh, God, Liesl! How could you do such a thing?" The grater clattered on the counter.

"What?"

"We are not beggars! We do not have to be beggars! How could you do that!"

"I wasn't begging! I was singing!"

She looked so angry, and I hadn't done anything. There were two bright red spots on her cheeks.

"I was trying to help," I said, "and I was working in show business and—"

"It was a terrible thing for you to do."

"No it wasn't! It wasn't terrible. It was fun, and you don't understand anything!" I'd thought she'd be pleased with the money and now I was being yelled at.

"Liesl. Do you remember when that one-legged man was in the backyard and he was singing and the people threw pennies from their windows?"

"He wasn't singing. He was playing the accordion."

"All right, the accordion. That was begging, Liesl."

"That was different. He was missing a leg and everyone felt sorry for him. No one felt sorry for me and Grace."

"It was not different! When you go to sing in a backyard for people to throw pennies to you, that is begging. This is something we do not do. Work, yes. Beg, no."

Mother and Father were always saying that. "We do not do this or We do not do that," with a big capital *W*. Some great big "We" making up all the rules.

"It was work, Mother! I'm going to be a singing movie star!"

"Promise me you will never do that again."

I was sure the people threw money because Grace and I looked so pretty with lipstick on and sang so well.

"Liesl! Promise me."

"All right, I promise. But it was not like the one-legged man!"

"Liesl, a singing movie star." She didn't look so angry anymore. She was almost smiling. "All right, I understand. I do. But be sure not to say anything about it to Father. It would hurt him very much."

"But Father was a singer himself!"

"Father a singer? No, Liesl."

"But you told me yourself."

"No, never. When?"

"Remember, in the Vienna Opera? Long ago?"

"No, no, Liesl. He didn't sing. That was when he was a young medical student with no money, and you know how much he loves opera. He and some other students would stand onstage in costume and hold spears for the crowd scenes. That way they could see the opera."

"Oh. I thought he did more than that."

"You are so disappointed, my singing movie star. No, I am sorry. We come from a family of shopkeepers."

"No actors at all? Not even one?"

"No, none at all. Not even a small one." She started laughing a little. "I know how you feel. You think you were stolen by the gypsies and put in the wrong family." Her laugh was so nice that I put my arms around her and hugged her. She smelled of carrots and lemon.

"Now you won't do that again and you won't tell anyone about it," she said.

"No, I won't."

She picked up the grater and went back to work on the salad.

"Grace Flanagan has a much better voice," I said. "I don't even sing that well."

"I know," Mother said. She was busy, with her back toward me.

"Why?" I said. "What do you mean? Do I go out of tune?"

"Only every now and then."

"Oh," I said.

"Poor Liesl. You will have to be just a plain movie star."

5

Everyone said it was going to snow soon for a white Christmas, and I thought this might be the last chance for roller hockey before the streets got slushy.

I shared a pair of roller skates with Hedi and she hardly ever used them, so we kept them my size most of the time. That was good, because we were always losing the key and the metal would stick sometimes and it would take forever to slide it to a different size.

Roller hockey was best of all because everyone played. Stickball was never mixed, and Chinese handball hardly ever. There weren't that many kids with hockey sticks, though, so the big boys let everyone play and it was exciting. We were playing, and I was thinking about how much fun it was to skate on the smooth surface of the street and how good I was getting at whipping around the parked cars real fast and—

Everything came to a stop and there was a police car and a cop getting out. I didn't know what was happening.

The cop was young, with a mean face, and he pointed his club at me. "You. What's your name?"

He had a pad and pencil.

My mouth went dry. I could barely talk.

"Liesl Rosen."

"How d'you spell that?" He barked the words at me, frowning.

My heart was beating so hard I could feel it in my throat.

"L-I-E-S-L." I couldn't talk above a whisper.

I knew this was an American cop, but there was a gun in his holster. The club and the gun, and all I could think of was the high black boots and the swastika and the menace I felt when one of them passed me in the street. If one of them had noticed me and had pointed and said, "You. What's your name?" . . . Shadows closing in.

The policeman had turned away from me and he was talking to another kid and I didn't hear what he was saying. This was America and the other kids were answering him in normal voices and the panic slowly faded and I hoped no one had noticed me. Billy Laramie was saying something to me under his breath.

"What?"

"What'd you give him your right name for, dope?"

"Oh." I was still shaken, like after a bad dream, and I didn't want Billy to see.

The cop's voice was barking, ". . . between parked cars. I shoulda taken those hockey sticks, too—you're lucky I'm in a good mood. I better not catch any of you skating in the street again. . . ." He went on and on.

"Yeah," Billy said. "If there's a bank robbery down the street, you can come here and break our sticks. . . ."

"You with the big mouth. What's your name again?"

"Bob Johnson."

"You better keep that big mouth shut, because I sure would like to bring you in. Bob Johnson, huh? You better keep yourself out of trouble. . . ."

He got into the police car and we watched him drive off.

"The son of a bitch," Billy said.

"Why don't you shut up? He was only doing his job," John McIntyre said.

"Who're you telling to shut up?" That was Billy, real fierce and fast.

I didn't hear the rest of it because I was sitting on the curb with Kathy Pages and taking my skates off.

"What's the matter with you, Liesl?"

"Nothing, why?"

"You went all white before. . . ."

I was pulling at the brown leather strap and I heard bits of Billy and John and someone else.

"Yeah, well, my dad's a policeman, so . . ."

". . . some Mickey Mouse . . ." Billy's voice. "My dad's . . . a lot of action overseas . . ."

"Oh yeah? Well, I hear your dad's a bum, big shot!"

I didn't see it start. Kathy said Billy's fist shot out and hit John square on the chin. I saw the part when John was already down and Billy jumped on him. Billy was punching and punching his fist into John's face and John's head kind of bounced. It was awful. Later, they said Billy had kept pounding John's head into the curb. There was a whole lot of blood. I couldn't stop staring at the blood, at the bright-red color of it.

Someone screamed, and then a man was pulling Billy off.

For a moment Billy looked dazed, almost as if he didn't know what was happening, and then his eyes cleared, deep blue and hard.

A lot of grown-ups were hanging out of the windows now.

A fat lady was yelling from the third floor, ". . . coulda killed him! Why don'tcha get out of here, you trash!"

Billy stood in the middle of the street, yelling back at her. "Mind your own damn friggin' business!"

I tried to remember what had happened, something about Billy's father, it had all happened so fast, and now John McIntyre was making a moaning noise. The scariest part was seeing all the hate and anger change Billy into someone else.

He turned and walked down the block, his head tilted to the side in that way he had. They were still yelling things at him. He looked skinnier and skinnier as he got farther away. I watched him go into the subway arcade and out of sight.

Even Hedi heard about it.

"And John McIntyre was bleeding so much and he had to have stitches and . . ."

"Oh, how terrible!" That was Mother. She was working on the pincushions. There was a pile of blue sequins for the eyes, yellow wool for braids, precut red felt lips. She had to sew them on the pincushions to make faces. I thought they were cute, but Mother said they were ugly. Gaudy. I couldn't have one, anyway, because they counted out the exact number before Mother got them and she had to give back the exact number when she was finished.

"And everyone said Billy didn't even know what he was doing," Hedi said. "He kept on punching him and then he took his head and slammed it against the curb!"

"That poor McIntyre boy. Is he all right?" Mother said.

"He's all right now, but only because somebody pulled Billy away. He would have killed him! Mrs. McIntyre said he's like a mad dog!"

"No he's not," I said. "It was a fight. Lots of kids get into fights."

"Not like that," Hedi said.

"Maybe he gets too mad sometimes, but he's nice."

"No he's not, Liesl."

"I think Mrs. Laramie has great difficulty with him," Mother said. The sequins sparkled against the dark wood of the table.

"I think he's nice, most of the time," I said. "Anyway, don't you think he looks a little like Alan Ladd?"

"No!" Hedi laughed. "Billy Laramie? No! Why, do you think he's handsome?"

"Kind of," I said. "Don't you?"

"He's the worst boy in the class," Hedi said. "He always gets in so much trouble. And he's disgusting. He's dirty and his nose runs and he never has a handkerchief and he wipes it on his sleeve!"

"It's not his fault if Mrs. Laramie doesn't give him handkerchiefs!" I didn't want to talk to Hedi about Billy Laramie anymore.

It was almost Christmas. Every time you turned on the radio, there was Bing Crosby singing "White Christmas," and on 181st Street there were lights strung across the street and twinkling decorations in the store windows and it looked beautiful. Even the five-and-ten had red paper bells hanging over the counters. I went looking through the Christmas cards and I loved the scenes: fireplaces and decorated trees and snow scenes and ice skaters and cute little angels, and some of them had sparkly stuff on them. There were perfume-and-talcum sets with holiday wrapping, and I wished I could buy an Evening in Paris set for Mother because it looked so glamorous, all blue and silver and starry.

Mrs. Hallandale was letting us rehearse the Christmas play almost every day, and at assembly we sang Christmas songs about boughs-of-holly and come-all-ye-faithful and I wondered who King Wenceslas was and why he was so good. I didn't dare ask because I was probably supposed to know. It might have been another name for Jesus Christ, like "Our Savior" and "King of Is-ra-el."

Every couple of blocks on St. Nicholas Avenue, there were Christmas trees for sale. I knew we weren't supposed to have one, but I ached for one anyway. Grace Flanagan promised I could help trim her tree. I hoped she had icicles.

The men didn't mind if I picked up the broken branches from under the trees, and after I had gone a few blocks, I had a whole bunch of little twigs and one good branch. When I came home, I put them on the radiators and the whole aparment smelled Christmasy. It was all right because a nice pine smell wasn't something religious.

One night Father, Mother, Hedi, and I all went downtown to look at the store windows. The best was Macy's. It was like a show, with jingly music and everything. There were scenes of going to Grandmother's house, with sleighs and snow, and then a roomful of children and grown-ups and presents and a glittering tree, and then one with everyone sitting around the huge dinner table with a turkey. There were moving things. The horses with the sleigh went up and down and the dog's tail wagged and the father's arm with the knife to carve the turkey went from side to side. It was wonderful. A man was roasting chestnuts over a fire, and Father bought a bag for me and Hedi. They tasted as good as they smelled, and I ate them too hot because I couldn't wait. We all held hands and the other people in the crowd around Macy's window looked happy, too.

Mrs. Hallandale gave us a composition to do on "How I Will Spend Christmas." That was a lot better than "Three Ways to Prevent Fires" for Fire Prevention Week. I sat down at the dining room table next to Father. He had a big, heavy textbook in front of him and I had a piece of looseleaf paper and a pencil and I thought about what to write. I thought and thought. I knew Mother and Father would find some way to give us presents so we wouldn't feel bad. I hoped for my own pair of roller skates. That would be only one sentence and I couldn't think of anything else to write. I chewed on my pencil. On the top line I wrote "Liesl Rosen, Class 5A1," and then I skipped a line and put "How I Will Spend Christmas" right in the middle in my best penmanship. That still left an awful lot of lines to be filled.

Father smiled at me and absentmindedly ruffled my

hair and went back to his book. I thought some more and then I wrote the first line, and after that the words flew down the page.

> *My father, mother, sister, and I will go to my grandma's house for Christmas. She lives on a big farm in New England with lots of animals. It always snows there by Christmas. Then we go on the sleigh with the horses and the jingle bells. My grandma is very nice.*

Father had told me that my red hair came from his mother. That was my grandmother in Warsaw, Poland. Everyone in Father's family lived there. Mother's family lived in a small town outside Warsaw. Father left Poland to go to the university. I chewed on the pencil some more and started a new paragraph.

> *The Christmas tree at Grandma's reaches right up to the ceiling. I will put an angel on the top. The house will be all decked with boughs of holly. We will eat turkey and sugar plums and Tip-Top cupcakes with all my aunts and uncles and cousins. There will be loads of presents for everyone. There will be a fire in the fireplace and we will sing carols. Then we might go ice-skating on the lake if we feel like it.*

I had covered both sides of the page. It was the longest composition I had ever done for Mrs. Hallandale, and it wasn't even due until next week.

Later, Father said that Mother's dream didn't mean anything. He said it was superstitious to believe in dreams. He said dreams were the product of your own mind's hopes or worries. He kept saying that, but I could tell that Mother did believe, no matter what he said.

We were finishing breakfast, and Hedi and I were ready to go to school. Usually Mother was up before anyone, but this time she was late. She was still in her green-and-white-print bathrobe and there were dark hollows around her eyes.

"I couldn't sleep all night," she said. "I had a terrible dream."

"What is it, Franya?"

Her face looked very tired and lined. "I saw them. I saw them all. My mother and father and the boys and Wanda and the children, even the baby. They were all standing and waving to me, smiling and waving."

Her hands were twisting and turning the belt of the bathrobe.

"They said, 'We are well and happy, you see, everything is fine.' Wanda was holding the baby up so I could see him better and she was laughing. 'You worried for nothing, we are happy, everything is wonderful, we have plenty to eat.' It was so real, I could have touched them. It was so good to hear their voices again. They were smiling at me, and then my mother said, 'Look! We even have oranges!' And they held up the oranges for me to see."

"Franya," Father said. He reached across the table and took her hand.

She looked at him with empty eyes. "It is over. They are dead. All of them. I know they are dead."

"Franya."

"How would they have oranges in Poland now? In December and under the Nazis?"

Before I went to school, I took the composition out of my notebook. I went to the bathroom and tore it into a million tiny pieces and flushed it down the toilet. I hated Mrs. Hallandale for making me write it, and I hated that big, happy family in Macy's window. I wanted to smash something. Suddenly I knew that Billy Laramie was full of that same hopeless rage.

6

The neighborhood was always watching. Mostly it was good, because you were so safe; if there was trouble, there was a grown-up to help. But it could be bad, too. Like for Jeanne. She was a fair-skinned, pretty teenager with light-brown hair and a slender body. She was in eleventh grade when her family sent her away for a while to visit her aunt in the country. Everyone knew, though. Even I knew, I don't know how, that she had gone away to have a baby and give it up for adoption. When she came back, quiet and slender, the disapproval was all around her like a mist. She didn't hang around with the kids on the corner anymore and she'd walk very quickly up the street, her body leaning toward the building line as if she were trying to duck the looks. Her skin was very white and there were some light freckles across her nose. I was sorry that her secret got out, and at the same time, I couldn't help staring at her, too . . . a teenager who had done That.

And there was Ann-Marie, the super's daughter, known as Ann-Marie Who Has Lice. When you played with her, other grown-ups, not even your own mother, would call you to their windows to remind you not to exchange hats or combs or get too close.

And Kate Laramie. The other women talked to her and everything, but you could tell she wasn't one of them. She didn't act apologetic like Jeanne, though. Sometimes I'd see her in front of the building, laughing and leaning against a shiny car and talking to the driver. Sometimes I'd see her all dressed up, wearing high-heeled ankle-strap shoes and swinging her purse and walking with a bounce. There was a lot of talk about little Mary being neglected, even Mother said that, but Mary looked happy to me. Well, she wasn't that clean and Billy had to watch her a lot and he'd be playing in the street and Mary sat on the curb and splashed her feet in the puddles with no one telling her to stop, and I guess that's what they meant. But Mary did smile a lot and Mrs. Laramie was always friendly to me.

Anyway, all that talk about Mrs. Laramie surrounded Billy, too, and then, after the fight, it got worse. Billy still played with the other kids, but the grown-ups treated him mean over any little thing and you could tell they didn't like him. The first time I heard the expression "white trash" was about the Laramies. I thought that was a terrible thing to say about a serviceman's family when he was away fighting in North Africa and all. I guess the Laramies not going to church didn't help, either.

It was one of those church mornings, the Sunday hush and the street empty. I was out in front by myself with nothing to do, thinking that having Hedi for a sister was as bad as being an only child because she was so serious and boring. Billy came out of the house and nodded at me and walked up the block, his chin tilted up like he was daring somebody to say something.

"Hey, Billy!" I yelled, and I ran to catch up with him.

"Hi."

"Where're you going?" I was half skipping to keep up with him and we were partway to St. Nicholas Avenue.

"Downtown."

"Where downtown?"

"I don't know. I might get off on Forty-second Street."

"Forty-second Street?" I thought he sounded so grown-up, deciding where to go without having to tell anyone or anything.

"Yeah."

"What are you going to do?"

"I don't know. Just look around. There's nothing to

do on this crummy block."

"Are you going on another adventure?"

"Yeah, I guess so."

"Can I come?"

"No, I don't want nobody taggin' along." He looked at me and his eyes were deep, deep bottom-of-the-ocean blue. "Anyways, your mother's not gonna let you go with me."

"She might," I said.

"No she won't. Not with me."

We were inside the subway arcade in front of Jack-andandy's.

"Billy, I think she will. I do. And I want to get off this crummy block, too, and—"

"Oh yeah? How come?"

"Because it's Sunday and there's nothing to do and I love it downtown. I think she'll let me. Billy, will you wait for me, just a little while, and I'll go ask? Wait right here?"

"I'm not gonna stand here all day."

"I'll be right back," I called over my shoulder. "Wait for me!"

I ran all the way home. Father was there with Mother, so I had to ask both of them.

I was out of breath. "Please, can I go downtown? I have to know right away."

"Downtown?"

"Around Forty-second Street just to look around and I have nothing to do and Grace Flanagan is going

with her sisters and they're older and we'll be with
them so it'll be all right and . . ." I was looking right
at them and telling this big lie. Why was I telling this
big lie just to go with Billy Laramie? ". . . and Peggy's
a teenager and they're waiting for me right now
and . . ."

They took too long deciding, and when they finally
said yes, I was frantic, thinking Billy hadn't waited,
and I ran all the way back to the subway arcade. I ran
so fast that my chest hurt. Because suddenly it had
become very important to be able to tell Billy that I
was allowed to go with him.

"Billy!"

He was still there.

"She said yes, I can go with you!"

"No kiddin'?"

"And I have nickels for the subway and a phone call,
just in case, and lunch money, do you like Nedick's,
and . . ."

When he smiled, his face looked so very warm and
open and it made me feel sad and happy at the same
time, so mixed up that I had to keep on talking fast all
the way down the elevator.

". . . Nedick's orange drink is my very favorite and
Teresa says they water it down and that's why they
have to call it 'drink' instead of 'juice,' but I like it
better than regular orange juice, don't you, and—"

"You sure talk a blue streak, I swear to God." He
didn't look tough or anything, though. Sometimes

someone can say something and the words by themselves are almost mean, but they smile at you in such
a nice, warm way and you can tell they really like you
a lot. Like Billy.

Times Square. It was the hugest station with a thousand different exits and people rushing in all directions. It would be easy to get lost.

"See those green lights up there?" Billy was point-
ing at the white tile ceiling. "Anytime you want to get
to the West Side subway, you follow those green
lights. That's the whole trick to it."

Billy Laramie knew just about everything. That's
what I had told Grace Flanagan once.

"You know when they say 'Lucky Strike Green Has
Gone to War'?" I said. "What do they mean?"

"Oh yeah, that," he said. "See, the package used to
be green with the red and white circle, and they were
trying to save ink or something. They took off the
green and made it a white package. They're saving the
green dye for the war effort."

"How do you know all that?"

"My dad told me. He smokes Luckies, too."

"Does he let you smoke?"

"No. I'll have to quit before he gets back. He'll make
me quit for sure. For my own good, though, you
know? He's always watching out for me."

All parents watch out for their kids. Billy was saying it like it was some kind of a big thing.

"He's a swell guy. When he was home, he did a lot of stuff with me, fishing and like that. Just me and him. I look just like him, too. Chip off the old block." He went on, bragging about fishing and playing ball and barbecues with his father.

There was a soldier and a girl walking in front of us. She looked pretty from the back. She had an upsweep and a cute little hat with veiling and her stocking seams were perfectly straight. He had his arm around her shoulders and her arm was around his waist. His head was leaning down toward hers, very close, and I was sure they were in love. I wondered if anyone walking behind us might think Billy and I were out on a date, too. I hoped so. I tried to walk taller and I wondered what it would feel like if we were holding hands.

We passed one of those big posters and we stopped to look at it. There was a big ship in flames sinking down into the ocean and you could tell there were lots of troops left on board. It was sad. The big letters said: "A Slip of the Lip Can Sink a Ship!"

"I'll never tell anything," I said. "No matter what."

"Yeah, yeah," Billy said. "What would *you* know?"

"I might overhear a soldier talking or something. I'd never repeat it. It would stop right with me."

"Yeah, Rosen, mum's the word." Billy was kind of laughing. Then he looked at the poster again. "Anyway, my dad's not on any ship."

"Are you worried about him?"

"Naw, not my dad. He's tougher than any-body. . . . Come on, let's get movin', we don't want to stay down here all day."

There was a vendor with gardenias in front of the stairs up to the street. Their fragrance was all around us and I thought it was wonderful, and then Billy said, "Phew! That stinks!" I was disappointed that he didn't like it because I thought gardenias were really glamorous. When I was famous, I was going to wear a gardenia in my hair all the time for a trademark, just like that colored singer, Billie Holiday.

We got out of the subway in front of the newsstand, and I turned around and looked at the Great White Way, only it was daytime, so it didn't look so bright.

"I love neon lights, don't you?" I said. "My parents took Hedi and me down here one night before the dimout and it was so beautiful, with all the lights and—"

"Yeah, it's okay."

Even without all the lights, even in the daytime, Broadway stretching out in front of me was magical. There were all the big movie theaters and a jumble of signs and the man in the Camel ad blowing smoke rings over the street and the sign that went on and off with the time and the temperature and there was a big palm tree for the Café Zanzibar. We headed uptown and we passed Toffenetti's and Jack Dempsey's and the China Doll and I stopped in front of a dress store.

"Come on, Liesl. . . ."

"No, wait."

The dresses were draped and sparkling and the mannequins were torsos, like dressmakers' dummies, and each one had a small printed sign: "Betty Grable," "Lana Turner," "Bette Davis," "Joan Crawford" . . .

"Let's go, Liesl."

"Do you think they're the real dummies from M-G-M Wardrobe, with the exact measurements and everything? Do you think that's really their dresses . . . ?"

"Naw, it's all fake. Can't you tell those dresses are junk?"

We went into the penny arcade and Billy took the longest time at the shooting gallery. He gave me a turn, but I wasn't any good. I got bored and tired waiting for him. He was taking forever. For a penny I got my weight and my fortune. My fortune said: "Patience will be rewarded." I started to show it to Billy, but he got mad at me for talking to him while he was aiming. I wished we had enough money to go into Ripley's Believe It or Not, but that was a whole extra charge. I hated standing around, waiting. There was a one-minute peep-show movie called *Forbidden Sin*, but it was a quarter, and anyway, I didn't think I wanted to see something really sinful. After a while Billy ran out of money and we walked around together, looking at the different games, and then we went out on the street again.

There was a doorway with a "Taxi Dance—30 Beautiful Girls 30" sign and a narrow staircase leading up. I tried to see what was upstairs but I couldn't.

"Do men pay for each dance?"

"Yeah," Billy said.

"Why? Why does everyone want to dance with them that much? Are they so beautiful?"

"Hey, Rosen, let's keep movin'. . . ."

There were photographs next to the doorway. Not of all thirty girls, though. There were ten pictures.

"It must be great, having your photograph up on Broadway," I said. "Millions of people get to see it, I bet. That's like being famous, isn't it?"

"Jesus, Liesl! They're whores."

"What?"

"Prostitutes."

"Real prostitutes?" I studied the photographs more closely. They looked like regular, ordinary girls, just like Washington Heights girls, even.

"Boy, you are so dumb! You don't know nothin'!"

"You think you know everything, Billy Laramie!"

"Yeah, well, I know a lot."

"Then *why* do they need green dye for the war effort?"

He started laughing. "How the hell am I supposed to know?"

I loved it when he laughed like that, from way inside. It made me laugh, too.

We started walking downtown again, past the Automat and the Strand and the Astor Hotel, and when we were a block from the Paramount on Forty-third Street, we could see there was a commotion and a big crowd. There were kids spilling off the sidewalk into the street and there was a policeman on a horse. Traffic was stopped and horns were blowing. There was so much noise and confusion, and then a boy walking backward went right into Billy.

"Watch it! Who do you think you're shovin'?" That was Billy, sounding mean.

I was glad the boy didn't answer. He kept on going, looking back at the Paramount over his shoulder.

As we got closer to the corner, the crowd was thicker and it was hard to keep on walking. There were groups of kids standing all around, talking excitedly.

There was a girl with bobby sox and saddle shoes next to us, and Billy said, "Hey, what's happening?"

"You missed him. He just went in."

"What? Who?"

"Frank Sinatra. He just went in. I was this close to him. *This* close."

"Frank Sinatra?" I said. "The real Frank Sinatra, right here?"

"Yeah, sure. He's in person right here at the Paramount. I seen him go in and out two times today."

"You're kidding," Billy said. "You wait around here all day? You must be crazy."

"I can't believe there's a real movie star right here."

"There's lots of stars this week," the girl said. "Frances Langford is at the Strand and Count Basie is at the Capitol with that dancer, what's-his-name, and Marie "The Body" McDonald, and yesterday I seen Rags Ragland over by the Roxy."

"So what?" said Billy.

"I got his autograph. Frankie don't give autographs. He looked right at me, though. You should of seen him."

I had noticed some of the names on the marquees. I had thought they were in the movies. "Gee," I said, "I never knew they were all right here in person."

"You know where you can see some stars? Waldorf-Astoria, that's where they stay. And Rita Hayworth's over at the Sherry-Netherland."

"Rita Hayworth? You mean she's there?"

"My friend saw her come out yesterday."

"Where is it?" I said.

"Fifty-ninth and Fifth. You know, by the park."

"Oh, Billy, let's go!"

"What for?"

"I have to see Rita Hayworth."

"Hey, you're crazy, you know? I'm not gonna go stand around all day in front of some hotel."

"Oh, Billy, please. I've got to. Please."

"No."

"That's not fair! I waited that whole time for you in the penny arcade. And that time at the Cloisters. That whole time you were looking at the armor and everything. I waited for you. And I didn't even rush you."

"Hey, listen, I don't want to."

"Then I'll go by myself." I started to walk away.

"You can't go by yourself. You don't even know the way. How're you gonna get back home?"

"I'll follow the green lights, the way you said."

"Yeah. You're gonna get lost."

"Then come with me, Billy. Come on. Please."

The Sherry-Netherland was in a nice place. There was a florist and a jewelry store with beautiful things right next door. You could see Central Park, and even though the trees were bare, it looked pretty. and there was a fountain and hansom cabs and horses and a lot of other hotels with uniformed doormen.

Billy was smoking and looking bored. I prayed she would come out soon, because Billy didn't look like he'd stay much longer.

People were coming out of cabs and the doorman kept opening the cab doors for them. He looked over at us once in a while. He was old and he looked cold.

"That's an awful job," I whispered to Billy.

"I bet he gets good tips," Billy said.

There was a little cluster of kids, me and Billy and two funny-looking sisters and a skinny young boy with blotched skin, and a very old woman. She was dressed in a long, black coat and she had a wart on her chin with hair growing out of it.

Her voice was harsh and husky. "Are you some-

70

body?" she called to a lady getting out of a cab. The lady looked startled and went into the hotel fast.

"I thought she was somebody. Didn't ya think she was somebody?"

"Naw, Frances," the boy said.

I was surprised to hear an old woman like that called "Frances" by a kid.

"I got Lana Turner, see?" The old woman named Frances was showing us an autograph book. "I got almost everybody." You could see saliva on her lips. "Bob Hope's in there. I'm gonna get him today."

"The only place I want his autograph," Billy said, "is on a check."

The old woman looked at him blankly.

"Come on, Liesl," Billy said. "Let's go."

"Another five minutes. Please, Billy."

"You keep saying that. Another five and another five."

"Next time I'll go anyplace you want to. I promise."

"What do you need to see Rita Hayworth for, anyway?"

"I just have to."

"It's too cold standing around like this."

"One more minute, Billy. . . ."

And then she came out.

There were two men with her and they cleared the way. She didn't stop for autographs and she walked from the revolving door to the edge of the sidewalk.

Her hair was bright red, brighter than mine, and

long and wavy. Her skin was creamy, with the faintest pink glow on her cheeks. It looked perfect and natural. Her eyes were large and dark brown with long, long lashes that threw shadows on her cheeks. Her lips were glistening pink and slightly parted. She was wearing a fur coat and it had long hair like fox, but it was beige with pale spots and it made a halo all around her. She smelled of something wonderful, warm and sweet and mysterious. Her arms were extended out a little and she wore long white gloves and she walked slowly, putting one foot directly in front of the other. And then the limousine door opened and she was gone.

"Oh, Billy!" I whispered.

"Boy! You'd think you just seen the Pope himself!"

It was a long walk back to the subway station. I walked slowly, with my arms slightly out to the sides. I carefully put one foot directly in front of the other.

I knew there was something perfect in the world.

It was hard to keep my feet completely straight. I didn't think Billy noticed, but then he turned to me and said, "You better quit it, Liesl, or you're gonna turn out like that crazy old woman Frances."

7

I had known all my lines for the Christmas play for weeks, but Edward, who was the soldier in my scene, kept stumbling and forgetting, so Mrs. Hallandale made us go over it and over it until it got completely boring. Some of the kids started saying Edward was my boyfriend, just because we were in that scene together. I'd have a boyfriend when I was a teenager, but it sure wouldn't be Edward. Edward turned red and squirmed every time I talked to him, and even though he looked good, for Edward anyway, in the khaki uniform, he wasn't at all the way my boyfriend would be. My boyfriend was going to be like in the Ipana toothpaste ad, smiling behind me with very white teeth as I reached for the brass ring at the merry-go-round. Or like the boy in the Angel Face ad where they were sipping soda with their two straws in the same glass. The boy had eyes like Billy Laramie's, but you'd have to like someone a whole lot to mix saliva like that. Teenagers in the ads did the nicest things. They were always on merry-go-rounds or roller coasters or at the beach or having ice cream sundaes, and they had those Pepsodent smiles.

I couldn't wait. I brushed my hair one hundred strokes every night and I brushed my teeth hard three times a day and they were very, very white. Father said to stop brushing so hard because I was taking all the enamel off. Anyway, I was getting ready to be a slick chick, a hepcat teenager.

Mrs. Hallandale's play wasn't hep at all, but I was going to do my best. The morning of the play, on the way down to the auditorium, I was feeling kind of nervous and excited. I was going to do it my own way and Mrs. Hallandale wouldn't be able to do anything, just the way Billy had said. I wouldn't stand in the center of the stage, all stiff and facing front. For my first line, "Welcome to Free France," I was going to walk over to Edward and smile at him. The second line was "We are happy to have a brave American soldier share our Christmas dinner this evening." I'd hold my hand out to Edward, maybe even touch his arm, and give him a long look from under my eyelashes. Then, when everyone was applauding—and there'd be a whole lot of applause because I'd be so good—then I'd see Billy sitting with Hedi's class in the audience and I'd flash him the V-for-Victory sign.

I knew that would make him laugh.

When we were finally onstage and ready to start, I could hear all the classes shuffling into the auditorium. I peeked out the side of the curtain and I saw the parents sitting in the back. Mother and Father, too. I knew Mother loved me a lot because it was uncomfortable for her to come to the school. I saw Hedi's class coming in, but I didn't see Billy. I saw Hedi and her friend Anita before Mrs. Hallandale shooed me away, but no Billy. Maybe he was in a back row someplace. I wanted to see his face to give me courage.

The play started with Alice as the American girl and the auditorium was very quiet. Then, in the Mexican scene, they couldn't break the piñata when they were supposed to and it took a long, long time and different kids kept on trying and the whole audience was laughing out loud before someone finally got it broken. Then the Swedish kids slid on the piñata candies all over the stage and Teresa almost tripped with the glögg, but that ended all right. England was fine and Big Ben's chimes sounded terrific and it was almost my turn. Edward's face was bright red and he whispered to me, "What do I say first?" and I could see he was sweating. All of a sudden I thought, If I change one little thing, Edward is going to fall apart right there. And then I thought about how much Mrs. Hallandale hated me already. I had never turned in the Christmas composition and I got into trouble for talking on line yesterday and she caught me reading

Brenda Starr, Girl Reporter when she was teaching decimals and if I did one more thing . . . Besides, Mrs. Hallandale was next to me, working the curtain and squinting right at me, instead of out front where she belonged. And all those grown-ups were only parents and not talent scouts, so it didn't matter anyway. . . .

The rope for the curtain got caught, but Mrs. Hallandale managed to get it open, finally, and the record of the "Marseillaise" started. I stood center front and said everything the way she wanted and Edward only stammered a little bit and it was boring and dumb. Later I looked for Billy because I wanted to explain that I did it that dumb way because of Edward being so nervous. I didn't want him thinking I was yellow, but the seventh graders left the auditorium first and I never did get to see him.

That afternoon Hedi and I walked home from school together.

"You were really good, Liesl," Hedi said from behind me.

We were walking single file because there was just that narrow dry strip on the sidewalk and everything else was slushy.

"Thanks. I know it was dumb."

"The play was dumb, but you were good. Honestly."

Sometimes Hedi was so nice. I'd try not to mind anymore when Father had those long, serious conversations with her.

"Your voice was good and loud," she said. "Everybody could hear you, even in the back. I was proud of you."

We got to the part of the sidewalk where the dry part was wider and we walked next to each other.

"Thanks, Hedi. I'm proud of you a lot, too."

She smiled and I thought how delicate her face was and how nice she looked when she wasn't so serious. We walked along quietly for a while, thinking. My armload of books was heavy.

"Was Billy Laramie there?" I guess I mumbled.

"What did you say?"

"I said, 'Was Billy Laramie there?' Did he say anything?"

"Didn't you hear about it? He doesn't go to our school anymore."

"What?"

"He got kicked out of our school."

"What? Billy? What?"

"Can't you say anything but 'What, what, what'?"

"What happened, Hedi?"

"He got in terrible trouble. You must have heard about it."

"No."

"Well, Mrs. Taylor was yelling and yelling at him, you know the way she does, and he started cursing and everything, and he pushed her. Anyway, she was on the floor and they said he knocked her down in front of the whole class and—"

"Billy did that?"

"Remember when he almost killed John McIntyre?"

"He didn't! He did not, Hedi!"

"Well, that's what everyone said."

"I saw it, I was there, he just got mad and—"

"There's something wrong with Billy Laramie, Liesl."

"There is not!"

"That's what everyone says about him—"

"Everyone in this whole neighborhood talks too much! Everyone talks about Kate Laramie, and that's not Billy's fault, and just because he has a bad temper—"

"Why are you always defending him?"

"I'm not."

We stopped at the corner, waiting to cross St. Nicholas Avenue. We stood back from the curb so the cars wouldn't splash the slush on us.

"Okay, we can go," Hedi said.

We went across fast because there was lots of traffic. That's where the buses turned around to go back downtown, and a doubledecker splashed right behind us.

"What's going to happen to him?" I said. "Can't he go to school anymore?"

"Not to our school. He has to go to a special school with a special troublemaker class."

"Oh."

We walked past the subway arcade.

"Mrs. Taylor gave us so much homework. I have to do three pages in math and—"

"Hedi, when did all of that happen?"

"What? The math homework?"

"All that trouble with Billy."

"I don't know. Last week. Before the weekend."

"Oh."

Little bits of ice that hadn't melted yet crunched under our feet.

"Liesl, do you like Billy Laramie?"

"How do you mean, 'like'?"

"You know."

"No. . . . Well, yes. I think he's nice."

"He's not. Afterward Mrs. Taylor said he was a rotten apple."

"Hedi, he is truly nice."

"You don't hardly know him, do you? Just because you think he looks like Alan Ladd . . ."

"That's not why."

"Oh, sure."

I shifted my books to the other arm.

"Liesl . . . don't like Billy Laramie."

I saw the best movie at the RKO Coliseum. Lana Turner was this society college girl coed and Robert Taylor was this real hard criminal, like a gangster, but very handsome. The way they met was that her college class was studying criminals and she met him in the prison or something like that. I wasn't too sure about that part of it because I went with Teresa and her little brother and that's when her little brother wanted a candy bar and Teresa said no and there was a whole commotion until she took him out to the candy counter. He got a Baby Ruth. Anyway, Lana Turner was so in love with him but she was worried about him being a criminal. It turned out that Robert Taylor was really a college graduate himself and it was his *father* who was the gangster and he was just finishing up his job or something. Lana Turner was a nice girl and a good influence, so Robert Taylor went straight and it all worked out.

Afterward Teresa said she liked Robert Taylor best of everyone. I said I liked him, too, but I liked Alan Ladd better. I wasn't trying to disagree with her or anything, I was only saying how I felt. But right away Teresa had to say that Alan Ladd dyed his hair black for *This Gun for Hire* and that any man who dyes his hair is a fairy, so I said that it was different for actors and it was okay to dye his hair for a part. Then Teresa said that if he was a real man, he'd be in uniform, and besides that, *This Gun for Hire* was on the proscribed list.

"There could be a good reason why he's not in the service," I said, "and I don't care anything about what the Catholic League of Decency puts on its list."

"I guess it doesn't matter if you care or not, because

you're Jewish, so you can't go to heaven anyhow."

"Well, I don't even believe in heaven and I'm going to Hollywood instead and that'll be when I'm young and beautiful and not when I'm all old and dead!"

So we got into another one of those fights and I didn't speak to her again until lunchtime on Wednesday.

Alan Ladd was still my favorite actor and Billy Laramie reminded me of him, especially the way he talked sometimes with his mouth hardly moving. I liked John Garfield, too, because of another movie I saw. It was at the Gem. He was a tough guy, but he was sweet to his mother and very good at heart and he was running away from the police, but it wasn't his fault. Then he met Priscilla Lane, who was a nice girl, and he was going to change his ways and you could tell that they'd be happy and love each other forever. They were running away in a truck and then the police caught up to them and shot John Garfield and he died. The last scene was a close-up of Priscilla Lane and she was crying in the rain. The sad part was that you knew John Garfield would have been a super guy if they'd only given him a chance. But he committed a crime early in the movie, so they had to kill him because crime doesn't pay. John Garfield was good in parts like that. Priscilla Lane was good, too, but not that pretty. If it had been Rita Hayworth, I bet the police would have listened to her.

* * *

The next Sunday I was out in front of the house, bouncing my ball and just hanging around, but I guess I was really looking for Billy. It wasn't as if we'd planned regular Sunday adventures, but on that day of Rita Hayworth I'd promised that next time I'd go anyplace he picked and he'd said okay and I wanted today to be the next time.

I bounced the ball and did "A my name is Anna and my husband's name is Al" for a while, but that gets boring even with somebody else. By myself, it was double boring.

Billy didn't come out.

I wondered where he would want to go. I was sure it would be someplace good. It was the sunniest day in a long time and the streets were all dry again and it was the perfect day for something really good.

I went to the edge of the sidewalk and looked up at Billy's windows on the third floor. He didn't know I was down here, waiting, and I thought maybe I'd call up to the window. But then the whole neighborhood would hear me, and Mother and Father and Hedi, too. So I went into the house and up the stairs. They smelled like soap and Clorox. Apartment 3B was the Laramies', the first door past the stairs.

I rang and Kate Laramie opened the door.

She was wearing a silky wraparound robe, black with big red flowers, and I hoped I hadn't woken her. She looked glad to see me, though.

"Oh, hi, Liesl, come in."

"Can I talk to Billy?"

"He's not home," she said.

"Oh."

She had very high-heeled pink mules with feathers on her feet, the glamorous kind, but some of the feathers were missing and they looked scuffed and a little dirty.

"Mary'd love to play with you. Come on in."

I took a step into the room. "Is Billy coming back soon?"

"I don't know. I don't know where he went. Mary's in there."

I had never been at the Laramies' before. There was a large coffee table with an overflowing ashtray and a bowl with soggy cereal and tissues and cotton pads and nail polish and a big red-and-white-striped box of candy.

"Here, have one."

"No, thanks. . . ."

"Go ahead, they're creams, they're good. Go on, help yourself."

"Okay, thanks."

"It's real chocolate, you know, the good kind. It was a present."

The couch had a pile of *True Confessions* magazines, and some clothing—Mary's coat, a nylon stocking, a cardigan sweater—drooped down from the arm. There were some brown grocery bags strewn around. I could see through to the kitchen. Dishes in the sink, pots and pans and a bread wrapper on the table, soda bottles and a newspaper on the floor.

"See, Billy goes to that other school now and so he's hanging out with the kids down there . . ."

"Oh."

". . . and Mary'd love to have some company. I'm real glad you came, Liesl. You could read to her or something. Just go right in."

Mrs. Laramie curled up on the couch with one of her magazines.

I went into the other room. Mary was playing with a doll, and when I came in she looked up with that bright, dimpled smile.

Mary's bed was unmade, with sheets and clothing and pajamas tangled up on it. The floor was covered with bits of crayon and comics and toys. I picked up a "Bugs Bunny" comic and moved some things out of the way so I could sit down on the floor with her.

"So then Bugs Bunny said . . ."

The room smelled awful. It smelled like Mary had wet her bed or something, but she was three and that was too old to be wetting beds, wasn't it?

"What does Porky do then, Liesl?"

"Porky says . . ."

Everything was cluttered and messy except for one corner. The other bed was neatly made with an army blanket tucked tightly into hospital corners. It had to be Billy's. There was an invisible boundary around his corner. It looked like the floor had been swept. It was completely neat and completely bare except for a photograph in a wooden frame next to the bed. I went over to look. It was a man in an army uniform and I guessed he was Billy's father. He didn't look anything like Billy, at least not in that picture.

"What's up, Doc, what's up, what's up . . ." Mary was saying, giggling.

I reached out and touched the blanket. It felt rough. I jerked my hand back. I felt almost as if I'd had an electric shock.

I finished reading to Mary as soon as I could. I wanted to leave in case Billy came back. There was something very private about that bare, sad, neat corner, and I didn't think Billy would want me to see.

8

Everyone said Viennese pastry was the best in the whole world. The refugee ladies thought it would be in great demand in America, and some of Mother's friends even went to baking school while they were waiting to leave Vienna. Most of them studied Kleine Bäckerei, the small things like vanillekipferl and creme schnitten. A few studied the larger, more serious things like Sacher torte and Linzer torte. The idea that the rest of the world was eagerly waiting for Kleine Bäckerei became a refugee joke.

Mother knew how to bake, too, but she didn't often because she wasn't a kitchen person. She did make poppy-seed strudel once. I must have been very little, because we were still in Vienna, before everything changed. There were huge, thin sheets of dough spread out on the white enamel table in our kitchen and they hung over the sides. Mother was stretching and rolling it, and she said it had to be thin enough to read a newspaper through. She rushed around to do something with it before it all dried out and her face was all flushed and there were damp kitchen towels to cover the dough. It turned out good, but Mother said it was too much trouble to ever do again. She even said herself that it wasn't as good as the poppy-seed strudel they had at Fritzi's. I remembered Fritzi's, too, in bits and pieces like a dream. Fritzi's was the coffeehouse on Langegasse where Father went, and once he took me along. It was very warm and had the deep, rich smell of coffee beans and other good things. There was a lot of dark wood and my chin barely came to the polished tabletop and I stretched up high and sat very straight. Fritzl, the owner, greeted Father himself and brought him his favorite newspaper, the *Neue Freie Presse*, before he even asked for it, and he knew exactly how Father liked his coffee, black with one lump of sugar. They gave me café-au-lait with Schlagobers—a huge mound of whipped cream—and I sipped the hot liquid through the sweet white clouds. The grown-ups made a big fuss over me and I felt so spoiled and lovable. Fritzl smiled at me with his eyes crinkling and gave me a Katzenzunge, which is a funny name for a piece of milk chocolate that doesn't look that much like a cat's tongue.

Father used to meet his friends there, and they read the newspapers and argued about politics and smoked pipes. And then one day a portrait of Adolf Hitler appeared on the wall and Father didn't go there anymore. The owner had become one of our enemies, and it hurt me to remember how nicely he had smiled at me when he gave me the piece of chocolate.

I hadn't thought of Fritzi's and all those Viennese things in a long time. What brought it all back in a rush, right here in Washington Heights, was the smell that greeted me when I came home from school. The smell—vanilla, cocoa, powdered sugar, apricot jam, all mixed up—was hanging in the air outside our apartment door and became more intense and mouthwatering as I came in. Mother was in the kitchen and there were baking pans spread out on every available surface. Her face and arms and apron had a light dusting of flour. The scale and little iron weights were on the table next to a large, thick book, *The Hess School of Viennese Cooking.* She was shaping little balls of dough and there were cookies cooling and more cookies in the oven: vanillekipferl, haselnuss busserl, marillen törtchen.

I ate a flaky crescent and reached for another.

"One more and that is all, Liesl. I need them."

"Why?"

"I have to tell you what happened." Mother looked very tired, but happy. "I made a small batch of kipferl and I took them to that bakery shop, Elstein's, the big one on St. Nicholas, and he liked them. He used the word 'delicious.' I looked it up later. 'Delicious.' He said my cookies would surely sell and to make several varieties. We set the price and I am in business, Liesl. What do you think of that? I am in business!"

Father was away studying with Dr. Koenig. Hedi and I helped Mother carry the trays of cookies to the bakery. Elstein's was four blocks away. We had to make two trips and the trays were heavy, but we didn't mind because Mother looked so happy. At the bakery the man gave her money and they shook hands and he was very nice.

When we came home, we helped Mother clean up the kitchen. It took a long, long time. Then she sat down at the table with a paper and pencil.

"Is there a big profit?" Hedi asked.

"Shh, Hedi, I am counting. . . ." She was writing some numbers. I saw a red burn mark on her wrist.

"No," she said, after a long time. "No, with the price of butter and sugar and the oven going all day and the price of electricity—no, it is not enough. It does not pay for my hours of labor. . . ." The happiness had faded from her face.

"Oh, Mother!" Hedi said.

"I will speak to Mr. Elstein tomorrow. We will have to raise the price."

On the next day, when she came back from Elstein's, the aroma of baking chocolate was still heavy in our apartment. Father and Hedi and I were waiting to hear what had happened.

"Mr. Elstein said my cookies were delicious and he

would be happy to keep on ordering from me." There were gray circles under her eyes. "He is a very good man and he would like to help. But he cannot raise the price. He says this neighborhood does not have the clientele for expensive bakery items, and he explained to me that commercial bakers don't use real butter and vanilla bean and . . . There is some kind of powdered substance that they use for eggs. That keeps their prices low enough and their cookies aren't so good, but still. . . . Maybe if I tried to sell elsewhere, downtown. . . ."

"No, Franya," Father said. "You cannot do this. You exhausted yourself yesterday—you cannot grind nuts all day; you are not a commercial baker. This will not work."

"I know," she said. There was a long silence. "When I think of all our ration stamps I used for sugar and . . . I feel like an idiot! I am so sorry!"

She looked so sad and disappointed. I was afraid she was going to cry.

Father cleared his throat.

"Franya, I have to tell you a joke Koenig told me," he said. "Some Viennese refugees were given entrance permits to Africa. They settled in the deepest jungle near a tribe of cannibals. One day the cannibals went hunting and captured an especially fat and succulent native. They put him in a large iron pot and did a ceremonial dance around it, and were about to light the fire when the cannibal chieftain said, 'Wait! I understand that a certain Hilde Lindenbaum is a fine Viennese hausfrau. We will have her prepare this succulent captive for us!' So they brought Mrs. Lindenbaum to the clearing and ordered her to prepare their dinner. 'Oh, I am so very sorry,' said Mrs. Lindenbaum, 'but I only studied Kleine Bäckerei!' "

Father started to laugh and Mother looked at him and then she joined in. They laughed so hard. Father hugged Mother tight and they were gasping for breath and she laughed and laughed until there were tears in her eyes.

I didn't think it was that funny.

One afternoon Mother told Hedi and me to take the empty soda bottles to the grocery and collect the deposits. I was reading *Silver Screen* and I said "Later," but Hedi gave me a look and pinched my arm. So we put the bottles in two large brown bags and lugged them down the street.

"Why did you do that when I said 'Later'?" I asked.

"Because Mother needs the money now."

The bottles were heavy, and I was glad when we got to the grocery. The grocer gave the coins to Hedi and she put them in her pocket. We started walking home.

"I heard them talking last night. After you were asleep," Hedi said.

"And?"

"They have hardly any money left. Mother needs it for groceries."

"Oh."

"You don't know anything that's happening, Liesl. You walk around in a dream. Remember the goulash we had last night?"

"Yes. It was good."

"Didn't you see? It was almost all noodles and hardly any meat."

"I know—I thought it was good. I like the noodles better than the meat."

"Oh, Liesl!"

Hedi could always make me feel childish. So I thought of an idea that even she would think was a good one.

"Hedi? You know that empty lot down by 188th Street?"

"Yes."

"There's lots of rubbish in there. I bet anything we can find some more empties. I'm sure I saw some."

"We could try," Hedi said. "When were you in the lot?"

"A while ago." It was a long while ago, because Billy Laramie was there, too, that day. It was before he was kicked out of P.S. 189 and started hanging around some other neighborhood.

"It's full of garbage," Hedi said. "What were you doing there?"

"Some of the big boys, Billy Laramie and those guys, made a fire there and they put potatoes on sticks and roasted them. They call them 'hot mickies.' They turned all black and they were pretty good, I guess, except for the burned parts and the raw parts and . . ."

We reached the lot. There was part of a bedspring and a rusted old baby carriage and a lot of paper and cans.

"If there are any bottles left, I bet they'd be way in the back," I said.

We waded into the debris.

"I'm glad there's no one here to see us," Hedi said.

I kicked over some wet, matted newspaper. "Here's one!" Then I found another one behind a cardboard carton. I was so good at finding things!

"Hey, Hedi! This is fun! I bet we find a whole bunch!"

"Fun!" The tone of her voice was so angry and mean. I looked up at her quickly.

"You don't notice anything!" she said. "You're lucky! You're so lucky to be so stupid!"

"What do you mean?"

"You think this is *fun!* Look at us! Close your eyes quick, Liesl. Close them! Now . . . do you even know what you're wearing?"

I kept my eyes squeezed shut. "My navy-blue coat."

"I know, I know. I mean, what else? What color is your dress?"

I tried hard to remember what Mother had laid out on my bed that morning before school. "The blue one?"

"No! The green checks!"

I looked, and Hedi was right. I didn't understand what she was so mad about.

"See?" she said. "It doesn't even matter to you! You don't even know!"

"Know what?"

"We're not dressed right! Your coat sleeves are half-way up your arm! And all our sweaters are European style with those dumb puffy sleeves! I hate them! I want a plaid skirt and a sloppy Joe sweater and a Peter Pan collar and saddle shoes and . . . Oh, never mind!"

I knew what she meant about the shoes. I didn't like plain brown oxfords either, or the woolen stockings we wore when it was cold. But I guess she was right, I didn't mind the rest of it so much. I guess all that was more important when you were in seventh grade.

"Hedi?" I said. "Why don't you ask Mother if—"

"I can't!" she shouted. "I can't tell her! They can't buy us new clothes!"

We found just one more bottle and I silently put it in the big brown bag. Hedi didn't even look at me.

I was thinking. I wondered if her clothes were why she wasn't one of those popular hepcat teenagers. I was lucky I was only in fifth grade, where being very good at Chinese handball and double Dutch mattered. When I was older, it would all be different anyway. I would have long, wavy hair and a fur coat like fox, but beige with pale spots and . . .

We left the lot and started walking slowly back to

94

the grocery store.

"Liesl. I didn't mean to yell at you."

"Well, you did," I said. "You really did yell."

"I know," she said. "It's not your fault."

We passed Elstein's Bakery. There was a birthday cake in the window with bright pink roses and gooey stuff. I was sad that Mother's cookies weren't there anymore.

"I know it's wrong to complain," Hedi said. "I know we're so lucky to be alive. I know all that. But sometimes it's just so hard!"

9

Saturday afternoon at the movies was the place to learn how you were supposed to be. A lot of kids were always there—with the big boys in the balcony, smoking and yelling things out loud—and you knew right away what was popular and what wasn't. Hedi should have gone to the movies more; she'd have learned more about how to act there than in all those books she was reading all the time. Okay. June Haver and Joan Leslie and Betty Grable were popular, because they were regular, like girls from the neighborhood, only prettier. Rosalind Russell and Katharine Hepburn weren't, because they wore those tailored suits and acted too smart. Everyone liked Maureen O'Hara. First of all, you could tell she was genuine Irish with all that red hair; and she had a real temper and spirit and everything. She could tell anyone off, like a pirate captain or even John Wayne, in just the right way, tossing her hair and her eyes flashing and everything. Everyone had nice warm feelings for old Barry Fitzgerald. He had the right kind of accent, because a brogue was good and made everyone smile. Other kinds of accents were for spies or stuffy old fogies. I wished Mother and Father could lose their accents. I tried to teach Mother how to pronounce *v* by making her say "velvet" over and over, but it didn't work.

Anyway, the movies were fun because if the picture turned out to be boring, the boys upstairs in the balcony made everybody laugh.

On this particular Saturday I was with Teresa and her other friend, Katherine. We were at the Gem and the double feature was *Road to Morocco* and *Once Upon a Honeymoon*. The Gem was a lot smaller than the RKO Coliseum, and some of the seats were ripped and smelled of mildew. *Road to Morocco* was like the other Crosby and Hope movies. Then there was a newsreel and the kids talked all through it, except for the part about the G-men, and then *Once Upon a Honeymoon* came on. Ginger Rogers and Cary Grant—da-da-da—starring in—da-da-da—*Once Upon a Honeymoon*! If your name came before the title, that's how you knew you were a real star.

Anyway, it was a comedy and Cary Grant was jumping around the way he does to make everyone laugh, so the kids laughed when they were supposed to, even if it wasn't as funny as the Marx Brothers. Cary Grant was supposed to be a newspaper reporter and it took place in Germany and Ginger Rogers had gotten herself mixed up with a Nazi by mistake. They were escaping and the comedy part had to do with the mix-up of Ginger and Cary getting stuck in Germany. There were those comedy lines and then, in the background, a little out of focus, there were Jews being rounded up. Someone was after Ginger and Cary and she was kind of giggling and she said, "They think we're Jews!" I felt my face getting warm and I looked around and some kids were staring at the screen, chewing gum and looking bored, and some kids were laughing. Didn't they understand the Jews were going to be killed? Teresa, next to me, was looking up at the screen and automatically sticking popcorn in her mouth and looking normal, like always, and there was a hollow feeling starting inside me. I wanted to leave, but I was frozen in my seat. There was the smell of popcorn mixed up with the musty smell of the seats. I was paralyzed, and the shadowy out-of-focus figures behind Ginger Rogers were supposed to be Jews being rounded up! And no once cared at all, and then the scene changed to a romantic one and I was able to nudge Teresa.

"I'm going," I said.

"How come?" Teresa said.

"I just want to. This is boring." My voice sounded all right around the funny feeling in my throat.

"You don't feel sick or anything, do you?"

"No."

"Oh, okay," Teresa said. "See you Monday."

We were with Katherine, too, so it wasn't like I was leaving her all alone.

It was still daylight outside and I blinked at the brightness as I came through the door. I hated that feeling, like having a light suddenly turned on in the middle of the night. I stood still for a moment, getting used to the sunlight, and then I started walking home along Wadsworth Avenue.

My whole body was stiff. And I didn't know what I was feeling, almost ashamed, I guess, and I didn't know of what. And I was mad, too. I would have liked to be really mad, but the kids at the Gem didn't know and I couldn't blame Teresa and all of them for not understanding. It was just a movie and no one cared at all. But Cary Grant and Ginger Rogers shouldn't have made that movie. They were grown-ups and they were smart and they should have known better. And I hated them for pretending to be beautiful and nice. I'd never go see any of their movies again, ever.

Wadsworth Avenue was very quiet and peaceful that afternoon, with just a few white clouds in the sky. And there were Jews being rounded up in Austria, Germany, and Poland. All over Europe, at that very moment.

During those last months in Vienna, Mother and Father kept talking about quotas and affidavits and visas. You couldn't escape to another country unless a citizen there signed an affidavit that you would never become a ward of that government. An affidavit was worth everything! But then, even if you had one, it was no good unless your quota number came up. Mother and Father were on the Polish quota because they were both born in Poland. Hedi and I were on the Austrian quota because we were born in Vienna. The Polish quota was very low, it was one of the worst, but Father had signed up early. Everything depended on your number. Father went to all the different consulates, looking too anxious.

The Dominican Republic was letting some people in. England was admitting children, but not their parents. The Swiss border was closed. The ship *St. Louis*, loaded with German Jews, wasn't allowed to land in Cuba or Florida; they were all sent back to Europe. Father said that when he went to the American consulate, the man in charge kept his feet up on the desk the whole time.

Father's friend Carl was arrested and put in a special camp. It was still possible to bribe his way out, so three weeks later Carl was released. He came to see us. He was suddenly so thin, and as he talked to Mother and Father, sitting at our white kitchen table, his voice was urgent and he spilled his tea. "Run! What are you waiting for? Can't you see what is happening? Get out!" Father and Mother listened and nodded because they didn't want to upset him, but later Father said there was no place to go.

Carl had been born in Poland, too, and his quota number never came up at the United States embassy. He tried to get into Canada. He tried Mexico and England. He never did get out of Austria. I remembered that he used to tell me funny riddles and he played the violin very well.

The Sterns also went from consulate to consulate. Monika Stern was my first real friend when I was little. She had long blond braids and we went to the same nursery school in Vienna. Our mothers were good friends, too, and we used to play with our Shirley Temple dolls in the park. She was a little bit spoiled because she was an only child. She had a thousand hair ribbons in colors to match every dress. At her birthday party there was real Italian ice cream and a puppet performance. She was mischievous and fun and she laughed a lot.

Her family had lived in Austria forever and they didn't know anyone, anywhere, who would sign an affidavit. Before we left, Monika went to Belgium all by herself because some nuns there were willing to take a few Jewish children into their convent. Later, Mrs. Stern got a letter and she cried. Monika wrote that it was a very strict convent, with vows of silence. It was cold and gloomy and they wouldn't allow her to have her doll. I could see Monika's face, scared, lonely, and confused. The Germans went into Belgium after we had left Vienna. Mother said, "Someone, somewhere in the world, has to remember that child's name, Liesl. You must try to remember Monika Stern."

I had walked six blocks from the movie and there were five more to go. On 186th Street there were some girls jumping rope, and one of them had fat blond curls that bounced in rhythm as she jumped. It was such a nice day. In winter you got used to freezing weather and then, when the temperature went up even a little, it felt like spring. A lot of people were out, kids on bikes and a lady with a dog, and the chant of the rope jumpers followed me as I went up the block.

I really understood a lot of things, even if Hedi didn't think so. I understood about the war and about how important the battle of Stalingrad was and about being refugees and Father needing to pass the medical boards. The thing I couldn't understand, no matter how hard I tried, was why anyone would want to kill Father's friend Carl or Monika Stern. And what I couldn't understand most of all was why no one cared.

When I reached our building, I didn't want to stay outside and I didn't want to go home and I didn't want to see Father or Mother or Hedi and I didn't want to talk to anyone. So I went up to the roof.

There was someone's laundry hanging from a line with wooden clothespins, a lot of white things and something bright yellow, and I ducked under. I was breathing hard with my mouth open because I had walked up the five flights of stairs fast. I had that private feeling of being all by myself.

"Hey, Liesl!"

It was Billy Laramie on the other side of the laundry.

"What're you doin'? Catchin' flies?" He meant my mouth being open, I guess, but I didn't even care. He had a big smile and his eyes were bluer than the sky, but I didn't feel like smiling back.

"What're you doin' up here?" he said.

"I don't know," I said.

"So what's happenin'?"

"Nothing much," I said.

"Seen any movie stars lately?" He was laughing, but in a nice way, not at me.

"No."

"That's it? Just 'no'?"

"What do you mean?"

"Hey, Liesl, this is the first time I ever seen you that you didn't talk my ear off, you know that?"

He was teasing in a nice way. I could tell. I smiled back a little.

"Something got you down, huh?"

"I guess so," I said. Billy Laramie was nice. I guess he was just about the best person to be with.

"You know what's a good thing to do when you feel like that? Did you ever do roof jumping?"

"No. What do you mean, roof jumping?"

"Come on, I'll show you." He walked over near the

edge of the roof. "Come on, watch."

I followed him. "Billy? Billy, what are you doing?"

He grinned at me. "Watch."

There was an air space of about four feet between our roof and the roof of the next building. Billy put one foot up on the edging.

"Billy, don't!"

In one smooth motion he pushed off and jumped across to the other roof. He stood there, laughing, his arms spread, his hair tousled. And in another graceful arc, he jumped back.

"What are you doing that for?" He had scared me and I felt angry and he was laughing.

"It's great, Liesl. You're like flying across and then, when you land, it feels good, you know? Like you're real happy to have something under your foot. Like you're honest-to-God glad to be alive."

"And if you don't land?"

"You go 'splat'!" He was laughing.

I looked down at the space between the two roofs, and there, five stories down, was the gray cement of the alley. And suddenly I was almost in tears.

"That's so dumb! That's about the dumbest thing you've done yet, Billy!"

"Hey, Liesl, come on. What's the matter with you?"

"Nothing."

"It's just a couple of feet, that's all. Sometimes I do it over on that other side." On the other side it looked like six feet across. "I know I'm gonna land. It's a good thing to do when you're feeling down, that's all."

"What if something goes wrong?"

"That's what makes it exciting." He jumped across again and his eyes were alive. He was so beautiful with the sky behind him. He jumped back and he was next to me again.

We both stared down into the canyon between the two buildings.

"Listen," he said, "you don't have to try it or anything. I'm not telling you to do it."

I looked at the distance between the buildings. It was no more than four feet on this side. "I could make it, easy," I said.

"I know," he said.

"I'm not scared, Billy," I said. "That's the truth. I'm not."

"Okay, okay," Billy said. "I believe you. Don't do it if you don't want to."

"I don't have the right to fool around with going 'splat' for no reason at all."

"Sure, forget it," he said.

I moved away from the edge of the roof and there was a fluffy white cloud drifting and the sun and shadows made patterns all over the tar floor. I might have jumped across yesterday and maybe I would on another day. I could tell Billy was disappointed in me and I hoped he would still like me.

I was thinking about Monika Stern and why I was

here and why she wasn't, and it didn't make any kind of sense and there was no reason. I had no right to go "splat" off some roof. I had to be something special.

10

The best thing happened! Father passed the medical boards! He found out just in time why Dr. Bloch had failed. The way Americans give tests is with a lot of true-and-false and yes-and-no questions. Well, Dr. Bloch answered the European way; for each question, he wrote a lot of things to show how much knowledge he had and, instead of answering just "yes," he gave different conditions and possibilities. The way Americans mark tests, they look for just one word, and if they don't see "yes," they mark it wrong. It was lucky that some of the men figured that out, because Father would have made the same mistake. And Dr. Bloch will do better on the next test; he feels less nervous about it, too, now that he knows why he failed.

Anyway, Father is a doctor again! The letter came while I was at school, but I knew that something good had happened as soon as I came home, because everyone looked so happy. After dinner, father went to Trovell's and got a whole gallon of chocolate ice cream to celebrate and he hurried home with it before it melted. The telephone kept ringing. Dr. Cohen passed, too, but Dr. Greenspan hadn't heard anything yet.

We had barely even finished eating the ice cream, though, when Mother and Father started worrying again. They were talking about what he would need: money for medicines, some new instruments, could he still use the old examining table from Vienna, how much would it cost to order a sign for the window, and all those other things to worry about when you start a new practice. It wasn't bad worrying, though. Father looked serious, but I could tell that he thought everything was going to be all right now. He had a whole different look about him. It wasn't that he was taller or that his shoulders got broader or anything like that. It was something from inside him.

I wished there could be good news without having bad news creeping right in behind it. Only a few days later, Father said that we might have to move away. The Jewish National Council gave loans to refugee doctors to help them get started, but only if they left New York City. I didn't want to leave New York City! I couldn't!

Mother said the reason we got this apartment in the first place, besides the fact that they didn't ask for a month's rent in advance, was that you could see our window from the subway arcade and so a doctor's sign would be seen by a whole lot of people. And the two front rooms would work for a waiting room and an office, even though that would mean not having a dining room anymore. But the Jewish National Council said that there were too many refugee doctors in New York City already.

Well, that's another reason we wanted to stay. Some of Mother and Father's friends from Vienna were here, too, and even if they lived in faraway places like Queens or Brooklyn, it was near enough to get together sometimes. With their friends, Mother and Father didn't seem foreign and hesitant, they told jokes and laughed, and Hedi and I belonged in a special way, too, even though some of the kids were brats. I think Dr. Greenspan's son, Alex, liked Hedi. I couldn't tell for sure if she liked him back or not. Personally, I think it's very boring to like your father's best friend's son.

The Jewish National Council wanted Father to go to a place upstate called Elmira. It sounded awful. Who ever heard of a movie star being discovered in Elmira?

Hedi was saying things like "I hope it's in the real country. It would be so nice, with trees and a house and maybe I could grow flowers and . . ."

I was thinking about all the things I couldn't tell Hedi, like Times Square and Broadway and going where all the theaters were and seeing Rita Hayworth. And even though Washington Heights was a whole different world from downtown, it was only a subway ride away. And then I had all my friends here, like Grace and Teresa. And Billy Laramie.

Father said he would travel to Elmira and look it over and then decide what to do.

I told Billy about it one night. I hardly ever had a chance to talk to him anymore because he was always walking fast on his way to someplace else.

We were playing ring-a-levio in the street, me and Grace Flanagan and some other kids. It was after dinner and the streetlights had already gone on. It was getting dark and harder to see, and then it started to drizzle, so the game broke up. I was running into the building and I saw him through the glass of the entrance door. There were double steps just inside the entrance, just before the hall where the mailboxes were. Billy was sitting on the top step, leaning against the wall, looking mad.

"Hi," I said.

"Hi." He hardly moved his lips.

"What are you sitting there for?" I was still out of breath and hot from playing.

"I'm locked out, dammit. I don't have the key and the bitch was supposed to be home by now."

I felt funny hearing him talk about Kate Laramie that way, even if she wasn't his real mother.

"She shoulda picked up Mary by now," he said.

"Where's Mary?"

"She's with this old lady that watches her."

"Oh."

"Kate's too busy screwing around to even take care of her own kid."

I didn't know what to say. He sounded so mean, even though it wasn't me he was mad at.

"When my dad gets back, I'm gonna tell him a couple of things and he'll kick her out so fast, she won't know what hit her." He was talking through his teeth.

I sat down on the step next to him. "She'll probably be back soon." Mrs. Laramie just didn't seem like the kind of person for anyone to hate so much.

"Yeah, she better be."

I hadn't really talked to Billy since that day on the roof. His voice sounded different, a lot deeper all of a sudden.

"I never see you around anymore," I said.

"Yeah, well, I hang out down by my school."

"Oh." I sneaked a good look at him. He was in profile, looking down at his hands and cracking his knuckles. He was just about the handsomest boy on the whole street. It almost made me feel shy.

"Do you like the new school?" I said.

He turned to me and finally smiled. "Me? You must be kiddin'."

"Why? Is it bad?"

"Come on, you know me and school!" That big

smile changed the whole look of Billy's face. "It's okay, I guess. It's a lot better than 189. There's more spirit."

"How do you mean, more spirit?" One of those campus movies flashed into my mind, cheerleaders and pom-poms and football teams.

"They have these rumbles and I'm in this gang, the Spanish Lords. It's good. They got a sharp jacket, too, only I don't have it 'cause I can't wear it around here."

"You're in a gang, Billy?" I thought of the fight with John McIntyre. I remembered blood on the curbstone.

"Listen, Liesl, you don't say nothin', right?"

"I won't."

"Ain't nobody's business." He pulled a cigarette out of the pack in his pocket and lit it and exhaled a stream of smoke. "Anyway, they got a lot of spirit. All for one and one for all. It's all right."

"The Spanish Lords?" I said. "You?"

"The kids down there act a lot older. The girls, too. They know their way around. It's a lot better than this dumb block."

"Oh," I said.

"Jeez, look at it coming down!"

We looked through the glass door. The drizzle had turned into a downpour and the wind was whipping sheets of rain along the sidewalk.

"I might have to move away," I said, "to a town upstate. Elmira."

"How come?"

112

"For my father's practice. My father's a doctor again."

"Good news, huh?"

I glanced at him. He was looking out at the rain. I wondered if he'd be sorry if I moved away. I wondered if he'd miss me a little bit.

"I don't want to live in some dopey little town."

"It might be all right," he said.

"It won't be all right. I really ought to be in Hollywood, California, but at least New York City is the next best thing."

"Jesus, Liesl! The movie star stuff again?"

"Oh, Billy, don't . . ."

"Hollywood. Rita Hayworth. Honest to God, Liesl!"

"I'm going to get dancing lessons or acting lessons or something, just as soon as we can afford them. That's not so silly."

"It's the way you say things. For somebody that don't know you, you'd sound pretty damn weird."

"No weirder than jumping off roofs or being a Spanish Lord!"

"Okay, okay. I can't tell you nothin'."

"Yes you can, Billy. You can tell me anything."

"They don't have no mick gangs down there, what do you expect me to do . . . ?"

"I don't know."

"So okay, go on, Liesl."

"Go on what?"

"We were in Hollywood."

"Oh, well, that's all. I was just thinking that the place you live in makes all the difference. If everything had stayed normal, I would have just grown up in Vienna, Austria, and been a whole different person, probably, and I wouldn't even be talking in English. And if I live in Hollywood or New York, I might be discovered and be famous and everything. Stop laughing. I might! And if I live in Elmira, I'll grow up to be a milkmaid or something. I was just thinking about how where you live happens by accident. It's not even up to me and it's not fair, because it changes everything about my whole life."

"I started out in Jersey and then I was in this other place and now I'm here. It don't mean nothin'." He shrugged. "Everything's by accident. Two guys in a foxhole, one guy gets it and the guy next to him don't. All accidents."

"My friend Grace says everything happens the way it's meant to. It's all part of a big plan. I can't believe in anything like that, not if people suffer for no reason at all."

"There's no big plan." Smoke was spiraling up to the ceiling. "You know something? I was the one that found my mother. She did her wrists at the bathtub faucet. If I'd come into the house ten minutes sooner, maybe she'd . . . There's no sense in wondering about it. There's no reason I came in when I did."

"Do you know why she . . . ?" I whispered.

"How the hell should I know? She didn't consult with me."

His face was expressionless. There was just the sound of the wind rattling the door. I didn't want to break the silence.

The dampness made the sharp smell of whatever the super used to clean the hall floor come up strong. Fat streams of water were rolling down the glass door. The step was cold against the backs of my legs.

"Liesl, we're in this great big glass goldfish bowl," he said. "There's this big, spoiled kid with fat fingers playing with it. He's fooling around and sticking his hand in the water and whoosh, hurricane. He overturns something and hey, earthquake. He got these pudgy fingers, see, and he's always squashing someone or breaking something, the way kids do. He don't care. He got a lot of other toys, too."

It was dark outside, and the light bulb in the hall was mirrored in the door. The streetlights were reflected distortions in the shiny, wet pavement. Far away there was a neon light on St. Nicholas Avenue, flashing through the rain. A car drove by and its headlights threw mysterious shadows all around us.

"It looks like a fishbowl," I whispered. "I feel like we're right outside the fishbowl."

"Yeah, we are." He was whispering, too.

We were all alone, just outside the world, very close. Our shoulders were touching. He was my very best friend, more than Grace Flanagan even. We sat and looked out through the glass and watched the rain for a long time.

Finally Billy broke the spell.

He stood up and stretched. "I'm starving and I bet you the bitch has nothing for dinner."

I stood up, too. "Do you want to come into my house?"

"No, that's all right," he said.

"You could," I said. "I could make you a sandwich or something." Mother and Hedi wouldn't say anything, at least not in front of him.

"No, that's okay," he said. His eyes flashed blue light when he smiled. He looked so nice. I hoped I wouldn't move to Elmira.

"I hardly ever see you anymore," I said. "Do you want to go on a Sunday adventure?"

"Hey, Liesl—"

"This time we'll go where you want. I promise."

"Hey, Liesl," he said, "you ought to know better than that."

"What?"

"You're not supposed to do that. You're not supposed to ask a guy, you're supposed to . . ."

My face turned red. I knew all that. I read the magazines and "What Every Girl Should Know" and all that. I knew all about etiquette and dating and that stuff, I didn't mean it that way, I . . .

"I wasn't asking you anything, stupid!" I said.

"Liesl, I'm telling you for your own good, for when

you get older. Some other guy might think you were asking him out on a Sunday date or something—"

"Oh, shut up!" My face was burning.

"You're just a kid, but even so, you're too forward, know what I mean? This time it's only me, but it ain't the way to act—"

"I wouldn't ever go out on a date with you, not when I'm older, not ever, not for all the tea in China! I wasn't talking about anything like that!" Just because he was hanging out with all those older kids, he didn't have to be acting like this!

"What are you getting so mad for? I'm just telling you as a friend—"

"I don't even know why I'm even talking to you!" He thought I was a drippy little kid, he thought he had to tell me how to act with boys, he thought I didn't know anything!

"Hey, Liesl—" He looked puzzled and put his hand on my shoulder.

"Get your rotten, filthy hands off me, Billy Laramie! You're just no good, just like everybody says!"

His puzzled look was frozen for a moment and then his face closed. It was too late for me to take it back. He looked at me and his head was tilted that certain way he had. I was afraid he might hit me and then he turned. I looked at the gray tile floor, my face still hot. I heard his footsteps going up the staircase behind me.

Later, I told myself that I had acted like Maureen O'Hara, getting mad and tossing my hair and all that.

Maureen O'Hara was always telling somebody off just before they got together. Seeing her show her spirit and her temper was what made the Western hero or the pirate king notice her in the first place. In the movies, it was love-hate-love. That's the way it worked. I tried to believe it had been like that with Billy and me, so that the sick feeling would go away.

II

It was a Friday night, so Hedi and I were allowed to stay up and wait for Father to come back from Elmira. He came home late because it was a long way by train, and he looked tired.

We all sat around the table and Mother put a cup of coffee and a buttered roll in front of him.

"They do not know what they are doing," he said. He sounded irritable. "The bureaucracy! They move people around from place to place with no thought of whether it will work or not." He took a bite of the roll. "Social workers!"

Father told a social worker to get out of our apartment once. I saw the whole thing. She was from some other organization, I can't remember which one anymore. She said we could have a loan, but we would have to move into a furnished room to save money.

Father was very patient at first and he tried and tried to explain that it would cost more to put all our things in storage and then move again, and besides that, it would be depressing and uncomfortable. She kept saying we had to follow regulations. Her mouth looked as if she were sucking a lemon and she spoke very slowly, as if she were explaining things to small children. I watched the little muscle in Father's cheek quivering and finally he exploded. "Fool! Idiot!" he yelled. "Get out of my house!" She left fast, almost running. It was very funny and exciting. I wondered if the same kind of thing would happen about Elmira.

"Elmira is not for us," he was saying. "I spoke to a Dr. Feldman, who was sent to a neighboring town, and he has been there two years and he is still not established. He says if your grandfather is not born there, you remain forever a stranger. We will never be accepted."

"Don't you think . . . ?" Mother said.

"No, it is not possible." He was slowly stirring his coffee. "I would have to drink in the bar with the local men and play golf at the country club. We would never fit in. I would not succeed in such a place."

Mother's head was propped up on her hands. They were looking at each other, thinking about what to do. Mother looked discouraged, so I felt guilty about it, but I couldn't help being a little bit happy. I had a feeling we weren't going upstate.

"What should we do, Franya?" Father said.

The coffee cup clanked against the saucer when he put it down.

"We must follow your instincts," Mother said.

"All right. Let them keep their loans! We try here. We will find a way to start here."

"Yippee!" I shouted. Hedi kicked me under the table.

The jewelry money was gone now. Mother went to sell the Limoges tea set. It was very old and it had been one of my favorite things to look at as far back as I could remember. It was fluted white china, so delicate you could see right through it, and it had little violets all over. The violets were deep purple and they looked real. They looked as though they were covered with dew, the way they grew in mossy places under the trees in the Vienna Woods, with that wonderful smell.

Mother asked me to go with her on the subway and I was proud that she had picked me. She carried the coffee and tea pitchers all wrapped up in paper in a big brown grocery carton. I carried the tray and the little things in another box. I was careful and serious and I felt very close to Mother.

We sat down together on the train with the cartons on our laps and I looked to see if she was sad.

"Do you mind very much?" I said.

"No, Liesl, it's all right." She didn't look unhappy.

"It's beautiful," I said. "I'll miss it."

"Yes, it's nice," she said. She was looking up, reading the advertisements on the other side of the subway car. I was surprised. I was going to comfort her and I was going to be grown-up and helpful, but she didn't seem upset at all.

"Doesn't this bother you?" I said.

"Yes, it does." She sighed. "I hate bargaining. I am not very good at it and I want to be sure to get the best price. I wish I felt more clever at it."

"But the violets!" I burst out. "Don't you care about the violets?"

"Liesl?"

"You're giving away my violets and you don't even care about them!" I felt my throat choking up.

"Oh, Liesl! What is it?"

"I don't know . . . I . . . ." It was hard for me to talk. A couple sitting across from us were looking at me and I was afraid I was going to cry. "The violets . . . you had it on a table, a dark table in front of the window, didn't you? And there were light-blue curtains and sometimes the sun shone right through. . . ."

"Our living room in Vienna?"

I nodded.

"And the tea set is a childhood memory? Is that it, Liesl?"

There was a piece of tape on the box. I was peeling it off with my fingernail.

"I bought the tea set when I was already an adult and yes, it is pretty, but I have no special attachment. But for you . . . ?"

122

"I feel . . ." I said, "I feel . . . like there's nothing left of anything I remember."

"I remember, too, the things in my mother's house from when I was just a girl. A big grandfather clock, a painting in a gold-colored frame, a tablecloth with red-and-green embroidery that my mother made with her own hands. And God knows where those things are now. . . ."

The couple across from us were talking to each other and not noticing me anymore.

"But it is only things, do you understand? People matter, Liesl, things do not."

"I know," I said.

"And so a tea set or even my mother's tablecloth cannot touch me anymore. I cannot care anymore." She nervously smoothed the side of her upsweep. "In the night I think of my mother and my sister Wanda and the baby and all the others and—" She stopped suddenly and looked away from me.

We moved with the rocking motion of the train and I studied the "Meet Miss Subways" ad. Miss Subways was a receptionist and her hobby was painting. A large Negro woman got on at 125th Street and sat down next to me. I was squeezed between her and Mother. The woman had the *Daily News* and there was a headline about a love nest murder and I tried to see the picture without looking too obviously.

"So, Liesl," Mother said, as if she were just continuing the conversation and hadn't ignored me for five stops, "so you see, the tea set is important only for the money it can bring so that we can start a practice and my children can have a wonderful life."

I nodded.

"And you will have a wonderful life, Liesl. You are a real little American already, aren't you?" She smiled encouragingly.

I smiled back because I knew she wanted me to. I knew I could never be a real American, like the kids in the neighborhood who had grandparents and family traditions and big Thanksgiving dinners where everybody came. I was surprised when I found out that Grace's aunt and three cousins lived a block away. Little Americans had relatives on the next block or down the street and thought all policemen were friendly. They didn't know the truths that I knew. They didn't know that grown-ups would kill children and babies, and I didn't mean maniacs or kidnappers, but normal grown-ups who were nice to their neighbors and took good care of their gardens.

We reached the 72nd Street station and got up.

"Now, please be careful," Mother said. "Hold it from the bottom."

It was dumb to have felt so weepy about the tea set. Some stupid china with violets could make no difference in the way I really felt.

Father put the sign up in our window where it could be seen from the subway. It said: "Emmanuel

Rosen, M.D., Office Hours 1–2 and 6–8 except Sundays." Mother always called him "Manek," so it seemed strange to see "Emmanuel" there.

On the first day of office hours, Father wore a white coat and the waiting room had neat piles of *Life* and *The Saturday Evening Post*. Father paced around a little and Hedi and I watched and waited and office hours went by. It was like preparing for a party and having no one come.

"It will take time," Father said. "You cannot expect someone on the first day."

The second day was like that, too, and the third. Father spent a lot of time sterilizing his instruments, and Mother drank tea. Father became restless and started taking little walks before the evening office hours.

He was on one of those walks when the man came. The man came into the waiting room at exactly six o'clock.

"A patient!" Mother whispered. "A patient is here! Oh, my God, Hedi, run down and see if you can find Father!"

We were crowded at the bedroom window that faced 191st Street and Mother leaned way out to look down Wadsworth Avenue.

"Where should I go?" Hedi asked.

"I don't know!" Little beads of perspiration were on Mother's forehead. "Go, quick!"

Hedi went, and Mother was holding the white coat

for Father to put on. "How can he do such a thing? Why is he not here on time?"

We heard the rustling of a magazine from the waiting room.

"What time is it?" Mother whispered.

"Ten past six."

We heard the creak of the floor in the waiting room.

"Oh, my God, he is leaving!" Mother said.

"Maybe he is just standing up to stretch," I said.

"I have to stop him. Here, hold this." Mother handed me the white coat and went down the hall to the waiting room. I could hear her offering the man more magazines, and her English was worse than usual because she was nervous. I could hear the couch as the man sat down again.

Mother was back and looking out the window.

"What time is it?"

"A quarter past six," I said.

We heard the floor creak again. Mother went into the hall where the man could see her and I heard him sit down again.

"Do you see Hedi?" Mother whispered.

I leaned as far out the window as I could. "No."

"What time is it? I cannot play cat and mouse with him forever!"

"Six-eighteen."

"Oh, my God! We're going to lose him!"

And then I saw Father and Hedi, running from the direction of 190th Street.

"They're here, they're here!" I forgot to keep my voice down.

Father rushed in and Mother was helping him into his white coat and she was so upset that she buttoned it wrong and then, finally, he was ready and went into the office.

I peeked at the man when he went from the waiting room to the office. He looked so uncomfortable and trapped that I was beginning to feel sorry for him.

The man's name was Mr. O'Connell, and it was good that we didn't lose him, because Father helped the pain in his back and he told some other people. Later in the week, Father had a house call for a friend of Mr. O'Connell's.

Father went to the big drugstore on St. Nicholas Avenue to introduce himself, because he would be writing prescriptions. The druggist's name was Mr. Rennhardt and he was a real German, but he had nothing to do with the Nazis because he came over in 1911. He remembered German, though, and he and Father talked for a long time.

Mr. Rennhardt started saying things to the people who came to the drugstore. He said, "That Dr. Rosen, he's a prominent doctor from Vienna, we're lucky to have him in a neighborhood like this, he was very famous, from the University of Vienna. . . ." I knew about that because Mrs. Flanagan told me. Mr. Rennhardt had said all that to her when she went in for aspirin. Mrs. Flanagan acted impressed and I was embarrassed and didn't know what to say, because it wasn't exactly true. Father was never famous or anything. He was just a regular doctor.

Mother said Mr. Rennhardt was doing that because he was a good man and understood our situation and felt a little guilty, too, because he came from Germany. So he was trying to help us. It turned out that Mr. Rennhardt was an excellent chess player and he and Father became very good friends.

Very soon Father didn't have time to play chess anymore—not with Mr. Rennhardt or Hedi, and not with me either, and just when I had finally learned how! Father was too busy for chess because there were always people in the waiting room during office hours and he had a lot of house calls, too. He didn't like the ones on the fifth floor because there were hardly any elevators in the neighborhood. He said, "My most important training for this practice was mountain climbing in the Alps." He said it with a smile, though, and I knew everything was going to be all right when I overheard Mother say we had next month's rent already even though the month wasn't even up yet.

12

We collected old magazines and clothes for Russian War Relief. We pasted defense stamps in booklets until there were enough to trade in for a War Bond. We learned the Morse code with black and white cardboard flashers to help the war effort. "Kilroy Was Here" sprouted in chalk on sidewalks and walls. Names that no one had ever heard of before became familiar: Tarawa, Bataan, Guadalcanal, Monte Cassino, Cherbourg. President Roosevelt was running for a fourth term against Tom Dewey and Marlene Dietrich posed in combat boots on a USO tour. And a year went by.

Some of the older boys in the neighborhood were growing Victory gardens in the vacant lot where they used to roast mickies. Teresa and I planted a package of tomato seeds, but nothing ever came up. The boys laughed at us and said we should have done something to the soil first. Billy Laramie wasn't there; he didn't hang out with them anymore. I saw him sometimes, mostly from a distance. He had grown a lot taller.

Grace Flanagan's big brother Tim was sent home from the Air Force without his legs. He was at Halloran Hospital on Staten Island. "Remember, long ago, when we sang in the backyards?" Grace said. "Remember the songs we picked?" I didn't. "One of them was 'Comin' In on a Wing and a Prayer.' I thought it was just a song. It didn't mean anything. I never thought anything could happen to him." She looked bewildered, as if someone had punched her hard in the stomach, without any warning.

Some things remained the same. "Office Hours 1–2 and 6–8 except Sundays" marked the steady pattern of our lives.

Hedi and I always ate lunch with Father before office hours. We'd come home from school at the same time every day and *The Kate Smith Show* on the radio would be just ending, with that song about the moon coming over the mountain. The news would go on as we were having soup, and Father would listen to it carefully. Then we had sandwiches and *Our Gal Sunday* would start. "Can a girl from a small mining town find happiness with . . ." I never found out, because that's when Father switched off the radio and we'd talk.

Then Hedi went to high school and it was just me

and Father and Mother. Mother was usually on a diet, so she gave us huge portions of chocolate seven-layer cake because she couldn't eat it herself. When it was time for Father to put his white coat on, it was time for me to walk back to school. It was a nice, relaxed period right in the middle of the day. Lunch at home was one of the good things about going to P.S. 189.

But then I started seventh grade at Humboldt Junior High School. It was all the way down on 177th Street. I took a bus home for lunch the first day, but I felt too rushed. From now on I'd have to have lunch at school.

P.S. 189 went through eighth grade, and I could have stayed there until high school; all the other kids in the neighborhood did. But Humboldt had a Rapid Advance class that started with seventh grade and did three years of work in two and a half. Father wanted me to transfer from 189 because I'd been getting bad conduct marks all along and he thought it might be because I was bored. And he never did like the principal.

When we first came to New York, they put Hedi in a backward class because her English wasn't good yet, and she came home crying because there was something very wrong with all the kids in her class. Father was furious and went to see the principal. She said something about Hedi's speech defect, and Father blew up and said an accent was not a speech defect and Hedi would learn the language from normal kids and he was a physician and he would absolutely guarantee that Hedi would do just fine. The principal finally gave in, but Father never trusted 189 after that. He worried about what would have happened to a kid whose parents weren't self-confident enough to argue. He would have sent Hedi to Humboldt, too, if he had known about Rapid Advance in time.

It doesn't matter now, anyway. Hedi turned out to be a super-duper student and passed the test for Hunter College High School. And here I am at Humboldt Junior High, all the way down on 177th Street.

The first thing I heard about was the Incorrigibles.

"When you pass them in the halls, mind your own business and keep your distance," Mrs. Letty, the homeroom teacher, said to us, "and you'll have no problems."

Mr. Klein, the social studies teacher, said, "I don't want any back talk from any of you. I get perfect order in all my classes, I can handle the Incorrigibles, so I can sure handle you. Got that?" And he showed us his "persuader," which was a long wooden ruler. I was pretty sure he was kidding about the "persuader," because he seemed nice, much nicer than some of the old-lady teachers.

Like Mrs. Griswold for English. She mumbled to herself a lot. "There are some terrible children in this school," she whispered, "and they do terrible things. Watch your personal possessions at all times." She was talking about the Incorrigibles, of course. She didn't know what to do with the Rapid Advance class either. She gave us busy work, a whole period full of underlining the correct word, "ain't" or "isn't," in ancient yellowing booklets.

With all that buildup, we couldn't wait to see the Incorrigibles, even though we were a little afraid of them. There was Rapid Advance 1, which took Latin, and Rapid Advance 2, which took French, and that was me, and then classes in each grade in diminishing order of goodness—3, 4, 5, 6, 7, and then the famous Incorrigibles. It was a much larger school than P.S. 189, and I was the only one from the neighborhood that switched over.

Being new isn't bad at all. I became so much more glamorous over the summer and, in a way, it's exciting to start a new school with a whole new image. It's a fresh start. Grace's big sister Peggy cut my hair in a dip and it looks great and I've developed a way of tossing my head back to keep the dip out of my eyes and it feels very sophisticated. I'm much too mature to still pretend to be Rita Hayworth, but my hair does look a lot like hers now and we are the same type. And just before school started, Mother took me shopping in the Young New Yorker department at Lord & Taylor's, and this is the first time I've ever worn junior sizes! We bought a jumper and a blouse with a keyhole neckline and a yellow Shetland sweater set and a navy-and-red pleated skirt, and best of all, a white angora sweater, which is just exactly what I wanted. I'm going to keep the angora sweater in the refrigerator because Grace told me that way it won't shed so much. Mother and I only had one argument this time. There was a wonderful jacquard sweater in royal blue, but instead of reindeer and snowflakes, it had the outline of two sailors with bell-bottom pants and a girl in the middle, so it looked as if they were following her, and on the top and bottom it said: "Hubba Hubba." I thought it was totally in the groove and Mother said I most certainly could not have "Hubba Hubba" written across my chest and I said it didn't mean anything bad, but she still said no. Mother's so old-fashioned sometimes! She wants to keep me a child!

I am a woman now. I finally turned thirteen, and I got my period at the end of August. Grace and I had a contest about who would be first, and it was me. I still can't believe that it is actually possible for me to have a baby. My period started in the morning and I was supposed to go to the beach later, but luckily I was still at home. I called Mother into the bathroom. I'd been waiting for it and I had the equipment all ready, but when I actually saw bright-red blood, my legs got all weak and funny. I felt myself slumping and I remember reaching out for the edge of the bathtub. Mother said I blacked out for just a few moments. I had never fainted in my whole life before. I thought that only happened in books and movies. I stayed home and Mother made a cup of strong tea and cinnamon toast sprinkled with powdered sugar. She said I could have it in bed if I wanted to. I really felt fine, but she said that, just this once, I could be pampered. So I sat up in bed with the big feather pillow behind me and Mother sat at the edge of the bed and we talked and talked. It was nice. Mother told me her first time came when she was twelve and that she was so startled and upset, because her mother slapped her. Mother was very hurt and upset even though her mother explained that it was an old Jewish tradition to slap a girl for luck when she became a woman. I can't remember either one of my grandmothers, and no one knows where they are now or whether they are still alive. I wanted so much to be part of an old family tradition, so I asked Mother to please slap me, too. She said it was silly and she didn't want to, but I kept saying "Please," and finally she did. When I have a daughter, I'm going to do that, too. I felt like part of a long line of women and I hope it brings me luck, even though Mother slapped me much too lightly.

The other big change is my name. The first day at Humboldt, one of the girls asked my name and I said, "Liesl," and she said, "Lisa?" and I liked the sound of it, so that's what everyone calls me.

Junior high felt so good, with the rustle of new clothes and a new name, and I even had highlights in my new hairdo because I sent away for a free sample package of Nestlé's powder rinse in a color called "Titian Temptress." It turned my hairbrush orange, but anyway, I felt like a butterfly that had just metamorphosed.

It's all wasted on the boys in the Rapid Advance

class. They're almost all shorter than me and they don't have any muscles. Some of them are supposed to be geniuses, like Kenneth in math, but they're not very interesting.

We saw the Incorrigibles come down the hall during one of the class changes. My new friend Olivia and I nudged each other.

"They look a lot older," I whispered.

"They are," Olivia whispered back. "I bet a lot of them have been left back. And anyway, those are the ninth graders."

"Why are they 'incorrigible'? Is it a dumb class?"

"A lot of them have been in real trouble," Olivia said. "This is supposed to be the last stop before reform school."

"Really?"

I didn't see all their faces because I didn't dare stare right at them, but a lot of them looked Spanish and there were some Negroes, too. The Rapid Advance class was in an orderly double-file line going one way and they were going the other way on the other side of the hall, with a wide space in between. They were supposed to be double file, too, but their line was ragged and there was a sense of something dangerous as they passed by. We weren't supposed to talk in the halls, but they were noisy and somebody was yelling something with the *F* curse in it.

"Some of them are cute," Olivia whispered.

"I didn't get a good look," I said.

"We'll probably get to see them every day. They came out of Mr. Klein's room."

Olivia and I just naturally became double-file partners when the class moved from one room to another, and I was glad, because we had a lot in common. I told her my favorite book in the whole world was *Gone With the Wind*, even though it was pretty old now, because I loved Rhett Butler, and she felt the same way and we wished there was a dashing, adventurous gambler among the boys in the Rapid Advance class.

I liked Olivia a lot. Grace Flanagan would always be my best friend, even if we didn't go to the same school anymore, but I could tell that Olivia and I would get to be good friends, too. She said she would eat lunch at Bickford's Cafeteria with me.

Olivia walked along St. Nicholas Avenue double time, with a skip every now and then. Her long jet-black hair gleamed in the sunlight. Everything she did, picking up a tray and silverware at Bickford's or counting out change, was done with fast, lively motions. I picked macaroni salad and Olivia picked tuna fish and we sat at a table near the window. We saw other kids from Humboldt passing by on the sidewalk.

"See those girls?" Olivia said.

There were three of them, with orange faces from pancake makeup.

"They look like Juvenile Delinquents," she said. "I bet they're those kids you read about where the mothers work in defense plants and they just hang around all the time and that's why they eat lunch out, because there's nobody home."

"Well, we're eating lunch out," I said.

"Yeah, but that's because *we* live too far away, but we have real homes and everything." She lived down on 168th Street, so it was far for her to go home for lunch, too.

"I'll bet anything you read all that stuff about Juvenile Delinquents in *Life* magazine."

She laughed. "Last week's."

"Me, too." I said. "Do you know those girls?"

"No, but I see them hang out with the Incorrigibles and they all eat over at the Automat on 181st Street. It's cheaper, but my mother says Bickford's is a lot cleaner."

The girls were almost out of sight. One of them looked like she even had bleached hair.

We came back from lunch in time to change for gym. I didn't know what the boys did for gym. The girls had to wear strange, loose green uniforms called bloomers. We giggled when we saw each other in them. The gym teacher was Miss Finley. She had a triangular-shaped body with the widest part at her hips, and her white hair was in a short, wavy hairdo that seemed to be stuck in some other time.

We had mental hygiene with her, too, earlier in the week. That was also a girls-only class, and I think it was supposed to be about sex education. She told us that women wore lipstick and pointy brassieres to

provoke men and that we should never do that. I had
never heard anyone like Miss Finley before. Then she
asked if anyone had any questions and no one raised
her hand, so we spent the rest of the period in silence.

For gym she turned on a scratchy record of "Red
River Valley" and taught us a dance. Two steps forward, two steps back, two steps right, two steps left.
I wondered where dances like that and songs like "Red
River Valley" came from. Miss Finley was like a faded
photograph from long ago, where you didn't know the
date but called it "olden times."

In double file, on the way back to homeroom, I said,
"I wish they'd let us do sports."

"Yeah," Olivia said.

"Or at least teach us useful dances like the rumba or
lindy."

"Oh, Lisa, school has nothing to do with the real
world, don't you know that?"

The class had left the staircase and was going down
the hall. There were hall monitors, so we didn't talk.
We were almost at homeroom when the ninth-grade
Incorrigibles passed us going the other way. The
Rapid Advance class kept its distance, hugging the
wall and even more quiet than usual. The loud noises
of the Incorrigibles seemed threatening, and even
Olivia didn't really look at them. We were passing by
and suddenly I felt a hand pulling my arm. I jumped
and I heard a gasp from the kids around me.

"Hey, what are you doin' here?"

It was an Incorrigible pulling me out of line!

"Hey, Liesl . . ."

"Billy!"

The hall monitors were calling, "Keep moving!"

He released my arm and there was a buzz around me.

"Do you *know* him?" someone whispered.

I was being swept along with the line and I turned back and he was already partway down the hall. We hadn't really talked since that long-ago time in the rain when I said all the wrong things. I kept turning back.

"Who was that?" Olivia whispered.

He was almost around the corner and out of sight. Billy Laramie went to Humboldt Junior High! Billy Laramie was an Incorrigible!

13

Billy and I were in the same school! That was an extra reason to get up in the morning. I got up earlier because I wanted to look perfect, and sometimes I had to change my clothes three times until the combination was right. I wanted Billy to notice how much prettier I had become. We were the only two from the neighborhood who went to Humboldt, and I knew exactly how it should be. Sooner or later we'd walk home from school together, and it was a long walk, fifteen blocks, so there'd be time for a good conversation, only this time it would be better and different because I wasn't a dumb little kid anymore.

I wondered if he'd carry my books. I wondered if anyone did that or if that was just in the movies. I had a big leather strap around my books and held on to the end and swung them. That was the hep way, not like some of the stoop-shouldered Rapid Advance boys with their big, heavy briefcases. I couldn't imagine Billy carrying schoolbooks at all.

I could see us passing the fresh cement patch on Wadsworth Avenue where they were fixing the street and Billy writing "B.L. and L.R." with a stick; when it hardened, it would be there forever. "B.L. and L.R." Then, in a while, we'd have a real date, and Billy would kiss me good night. I'd close my eyes and be very passionate. I hadn't ever been kissed yet, and it was time. Olivia had had her first kiss already; she told me about it—it was in July. It was a friend of her brother's and it happened in Rockaway, when her family was there for the month, but he lived in Brooklyn, so she never saw him again. Olivia was ahead of me and I wanted to catch up. My first kiss would be Billy because that was the way it was supposed to be.

The Incorrigibles passed us in the hall every day when they came out of Mr. Klein's room. Mr. Klein's was their homeroom. They passed us right on schedule, when we were on the way up to French, and Olivia and I both looked for Billy. Billy was on the wrong side of the line, away from me, near the wall. He was kidding around with a boy with a flat, hard face and he didn't even see me.

"Hi, Billy," I called softly.

He glanced up and nodded, and the line moved on.

"Gee, he's cute," Olivia said.

"I know," I said.

"He's got the bluest eyes," Olivia said. "I noticed that right away."

"He always did. They're cornflower blue," I said.

"Yeah. Most blue eyes are more watery-looking."

"He could have said something."

"Well, the line was moving and everything. You can't blame him, Lisa. . . ."

The hall monitor saw us. "You there! Stop talking!"

I knew a moving line or a hall monitor would never have stopped Billy if he had wanted to say something to me.

I felt out of place in the junior high bathroom because the Incorrigible girls hung out there, combing their hair and smoking and looking everyone over. Those girls were tough, and once there was a funny, sweet smell mixed in with the smoke and someone laughed and said it was called Mary Jane. I'd see their lipstick scrawls on the walls. "My love has a big one" in scarlet on white tile. I felt embarrassed reading that. Even if she was doing It, how could someone go and write that on a wall? There were lots of hearts and initials. Then a statement appeared. "I like Luis but just as a friend." Who cared? Periodically the marks disappeared, and then the wall would fill up with new ones. One day one of the new ones, written in large blue letters, was "Me and Bill Laramie." I was surprised by how bad that made me feel. At the same time, I was glad it said "Bill." I was the only one who knew he was really "Billy."

Most of the time I used the bathroom at Bickford's, but once I was washing my hands at school and trying to be inconspicuous and get out of there quickly. I heard someone behind me giggling, "Laramie says he's going . . ." and then someone else said, "Hey, hey, Mona!" and there was more giggling. I looked to see who Mona was. I could see them in the mirror. There was a group of girls, leaning against the wastepaper container and smoking and laughing. They were saying other things about "Laramie" and the one called Mona was in the center of it. There was something about the way she said just his last name and took her time with each syllable, with her voice all throaty. She had long brown hair in a pageboy and bright-red lipstick that went past her upper lip to make square corners. She was wearing a black lace blouse. I had seen her in a stairwell once, between classes, kissing a boy in a black-and-white lumber jacket.

I thought those girls were probably Juvenile Delinquents or V-girls. I read about V-girls in *Life* magazine. V was short for Victory. *Life* said there were khaki-wacky teenage girls who picked up servicemen and slept with them for free because they thought they were helping the war effort and boosting morale, but actually they were spreading all kinds of diseases. *Life* said some were as young as thirteen. Mona looked older, though. She had a pretty face. I had the feeling she was the "me" in "Me and Bill Laramie."

I saw her with him after school. There was a luncheonette up the block from the school yard and Billy was slouched out in front with Mona and those girls, and some boys in the orange Spanish Lords jackets. I passed by very slowly and he had plenty of time to catch up to me or call me over, but he didn't. I said "Hello" and he mumbled "Hello" back. He looked like he hardly knew me and kept right on talking to somebody.

I had walked right by Billy and he never even thought of walking home with me! He just stood there with his Lucky Strikes and his Incorrigibles! I wasn't going to like him anymore. I thought a lot about how much I didn't like him, especially when I was in Mr. Klein's social studies class, because that was Billy's homeroom and I'd wonder which seat was his.

During fourth period one day, I volunteered to take a folder down to the office from Mrs. Griswold. After I delivered it, I took my time going back up.

I was on the staircase between the first and second floors when I saw him. He was a skinny boy with very bad skin and he was sitting cross-legged on the floor of the landing. I felt funny about passing him. He was taking up an awful lot of room.

"Excuse me," I said. I was two steps down from the landing.

He grinned up at me and didn't move.

"Excuse me," I said.

"Sure, go ahead." He got up and he was standing now, but he still hadn't moved out of the way.

I would have to squeeze by him. I hesitated. I didn't like the way he was smiling, but I wasn't afraid, just uncomfortable. He was shorter than me and very skinny.

"Can you get out of my way?" I said.

"Why you want me to do that, eh?" he said. "Come on up."

I went up to the landing and was going by fast when he grabbed my arm. I tried to pull away, but he was grinning at me and pulling me close and I could suddenly feel my heart beating fast. I was pulling away as hard as I could and there wasn't a word between us. He was grabbing at my blouse and I couldn't pull away.

"Let her go." It was Billy, coming up the stairs below me.

"Hey, Bill . . ."

"I know her."

"I was just fooling around. . . ."

"Yeah."

"Okay, what's the big deal, eh?" He was holding my arm and he watched Billy coming up the stairs below us. He didn't look at me at all. He was staring at Billy, and Billy stopped on the stairs and stared up at him. No one moved.

"Come on, I know her," Billy said. He sounded cautious.

146

There was a pause, no one moving. And then the boy shrugged. "Okay, okay, I was just havin' some fun." He went up a flight and out through the hall door. The hall door was swinging in smaller and smaller arcs and then stopped.

My legs had started feeling shaky.

Billy was up to the landing. "What're you hangin' around here for?"

"I'm not hanging around! I was doing an errand."

"Yeah, well, you could have found yourself a whole lot of trouble."

"I was all right," I said.

"Jesus! I know that guy. There's something wrong with him—"

"I could have handled it," I said. My voice came out shaky and not the way I wanted it.

"Sure you could!" He sounded mad.

"I could have. He was so skinny and short and—"

"He carries a shiv, okay?"

"A what?"

"Shiv! Knife!"

"Oh," I said.

He was going up the stairs ahead of me. "Come on, let's go!"

"Thanks, Billy," I whispered to his back, following him.

"Yeah, yeah." Suddenly he wheeled around on the stairs and faced me. "Do yourself a favor, will you, and go buy yourself a bra!" He was yelling at me.

"What?"

"Every goddamn thing shows through that shirt!"

I felt my face getting hot. I was wearing my new keyhole-neckline blouse and it wasn't even sheer or anything. "It does not! You're crazy!" I tried to tuck it back into my skirt where it had been pulled out.

"Yeah. You want every goddamn pervert in this school to feel you up, that's okay with me."

"Terrific, Laramie." My face was red-hot. "Is that the way you always talk to girls?"

"No. That's the way I talk to you."

"Well, I don't like it."

"Good. Then don't talk to me no more. You always talk too damn much, anyway."

"I haven't talked to you in years!"

"I was telling you for your own good, okay? Watch yourself."

He turned around and kept going up, and when he got to the top landing, I caught up with him.

"Well, I'll tell you something for your own good, Billy Laramie!"

"Yeah? What's that?"

"You're gonna wind up getting V.D. or something."

"What? What did you say?"

"From Mona and those J.D. girls. So you watch *your* self."

"Oh, Jesus!" He was laughing.

My face must have been crimson by now. "Over

thirty percent of J.D. girls have V.D."

"What the hell do you know about V.D.?" He was still laughing.

"It said so in *Life.*"

"Terrific, Rosen—is that the way you always talk to boys?"

"No. That's the way I talk to you."

"You know something? I think you got a screw loose, honest to God."

He swung up the next flight of stairs and then, just before he disappeared around the corner, he yelled down to me, "And cut out the Rita Hayworth walk! You know what you look like?"

"That's how much you know, Billy Laramie! I haven't even *been* Rita Hayworth in years!" He was gone and I couldn't tell if he had heard me. I could hear his laughter trailing behind him.

14

Billy Laramie was crazy. I wasn't busty at all. That was the most obvious difference between me and Rita Hayworth. I was only thirteen, though, so there was still lots of hope.

"Hedi, do you think I need a bra?"

"What?" Hedi reluctantly looked up from the book she was reading.

"Do you think I should wear a bra?" I suddenly felt shy.

"You could," she said. "You're old enough."

"Does anything show?"

She looked at me critically. "A little, not much. But if you're going to wear sweaters . . ."

So Olivia and I made our purchases together the next afternoon after school. We looked both ways down the street to make sure no one we knew was around before we went into Milady Lingerie.

I wanted a black lace bra because I thought black lace was the most alluring, but Olivia said no, because it would show right through our clothes.

"That's only for under black tops," Olivia said.

"I wish I could have a black blouse, but my mother won't let me," I said. "My mother says I'm too young! Can you imagine, as if it had anything to do with age!"

"How old do you have to be?"

"I don't know. Who knows, maybe sixteen!" That was another one of Mother's silly European traditions that were holding me back from my true sexiness.

We bought matching white lace bras. The lace was itchy against my skin, but plain white cotton was too boring. We were very giggly, walking down the street, knowing what was in the pink paper bags we were carrying.

I started wearing mine all the time, and one day when we passed the Incorrigibles in the hall, Billy looked right at my chest and grinned and held up his thumb and forefinger in a circle in the okay sign.

"It's not because of anything *you* said, you jerk," I hissed at him.

He laughed right out loud and the kids in line near me looked at me funny. Even Olivia. And then the lines passed by.

"What was that about?" Olivia asked.

"Oh, nothing!" I wished my skin were olive so blushing wouldn't show as much.

"If you like him," Olivia said, "you ought to try to be nicer."

"I am nice."

"You just called him a jerk, Lisa."

"Anyway, I don't like him anymore."

"You do too!"

"I hate him."

"I always tell you the truth, Lisa." She looked hurt. "I even told you I like Larry Cramer."

Larry Cramer was supposed to be the best-looking boy in Rapid Advance, but he was short and his eyes were too small and I couldn't understand how Olivia could really like him. He wasn't anywhere near as manly and handsome as Billy Laramie. Larry Cramer was more like the Roddy McDowall type. The more I thought about it, the more I thought I should give Billy one more chance.

Every third Friday night, there was a dance in Humboldt's gym. It was part of the keep-the-kids-off-the-streets campaign against Juvenile Delinquency, and a community group contributed punch and cookies. I heard that the Incorrigibles went to those things. Most of the time, I'd see them hanging out in a big group in front of the luncheonette near the school yard, and on those third Friday nights, I guess they just went indoors. I couldn't understand why it should make so much difference to anyone whether they were on the street or in the gym.

The Rapid Advance kids never went to those dances. Mostly we went to parties in people's houses, where the boys stood around by themselves, looking at the girls and eating all the little sandwiches. They were boring. I went to a party at Ellen Feldman's and everyone started playing post office and I thought it was immature. Olivia went into the closet with Larry Cramer for the longest time, though.

Anyway, the third Friday night of the month was coming up again, and I started thinking that if I went to the dance, maybe Billy would be there and then he'd come over and the music would be playing and . . .

"Olivia, let's go, this Friday, okay?"

"We don't know any of those kids."

"I know Billy, and you think some of those boys are cute. You know you do."

"But we don't *know* them."

"You can't get to know them just passing by in school, but at a dance, Olivia, it would be so easy for one of the cute ones to ask you to dance and—"

"I don't know, Lisa."

"Oh, come on, please. If we don't like it, we can always leave. Oh, come on, Olivia. . . . Just to keep me company?"

"Okay, but I honestly think we'll feel very funny there. . . ."

I thought for a long time about what to wear, because I wanted Billy to see me looking new and different. There was a movie where June Allyson was a tomboy and Van Johnson had never even noticed she was a girl, but then the night of the prom she was all dressed up in a long white gown, and when she came down the long staircase, Van Johnson's mouth opened in amazement and he stared and stared at her and in the background, violins started playing.

I decided to wear my brand-new blouse, white, in a silky fabric, with a Peter Pan collar and very full, long sleeves. I borrowed Hedi's pearl necklace. I had bought light-gray eyeshadow called Misty Pearl and lipstick called Glow Pink. I felt pearlized and feminine.

Olivia and I met a block away from the school so that we could walk in together. We could hear a record playing as we came in through the gym door. It was "Is You Is or Is You Ain't My Baby."

"After all this," I said, "I hope Billy's here."

"If he's not," Olivia said, "there are a lot of other cute Incorrigibles."

Olivia didn't understand. I wouldn't like any other Incorrigibles. If I didn't know Billy so well, I'd probably be afraid of him.

There was a metal table with a pitcher of juice and a plate of cookies on the far side of the room. It was surrounded by the regular luncheonette group—some Spanish Lords and some other Incorrigibles. Billy was there, and Mona, too.

Olivia and I were the only outsiders.

The Andrews Sisters' record of "Boogie-Woogie Bugle Boy of Company B" went on, and two couples started dancing. They didn't do the lindy the way I knew how. They put in a lot of extra steps and they were good.

Except for the ones doing the lindy, everyone was standing around in one big, tight group, talking.

"I didn't know it would be only that one crowd," I whispered.

"Boy, are we out of place!" Olivia said.

"I thought there'd be some other people, too."

"Well, it's just us and them."

"Do you think he'll see me?"

"Lisa, the whole gym is empty. He can't help seeing you."

Billy was talking to someone. I didn't think he had noticed me yet.

"I guess we could walk over to the punch," I said.

"We could," Olivia said.

"Let's wait awhile, though," I said. I'd have to get all my confidence together to walk all the way across the room and into the middle of those kids.

The Andrews Sisters ended and Xavier Cugat's record of "Bésame Mucho" went on. A lot of couples started dancing.

I had learned how to do the rumba a long time ago, when I sent away for the Arthur Murray sheets. There were printed footsteps to follow. The rumba I knew about was a box step in rhythm. These kids were doing something else.

"What is that? What are they doing?" In case Billy asked me to dance, I'd have to know what to do.

"The Cuban rumba," Olivia said. "It's not hard. You just don't move very much."

"Oh," I said.

They were hardly moving their feet at all. Their hips were swaying in rhythm and they weren't even in regular dance position. The boys had their arms tight around the girls' waists and the girls had both arms around the boys' necks.

I watched them and I knew I looked like a little kid, like a baby, with that Peter Pan collar. I wished I had a dress like Mona's—draped, sexy, with a low neckline.

Then Billy and Mona were dancing. They were dancing like everybody else, their hips swaying, pasted together, and they stayed in one spot the whole time. They were just shifting weight back and forth in the same place. I didn't know Billy could dance. And he was kissing her neck and it looked like he and Mona were really together and it wasn't just some scribbling on the bathroom wall.

At some point his eyes flicked over in my direction and I knew he saw me because he looked surprised, and then his eyes flicked away.

I watched Billy and Mona. I watched numbly. I couldn't look away. It went on and on.

Olivia touched my arm. "We might as well go."

Her words finally released me.

I walked home by myself in the quiet dark. It was a soft night. I thought I could still hear "Bésame Mucho" in the distance. It sounded passionate and aching and lonely all at the same time. I tried to hum along and my throat choked around it. Billy was living a whole separate life that I knew nothing about. He had cheated me out of my happy ending.

15

I was going to the Alder-Norman Studio in Carnegie Hall for drama lessons!

I had been waiting so long. First, we couldn't afford it, and then, when we could, I had to wait until I was thirteen. The Alder-Norman Studio didn't accept anyone younger than teenage, and in the meantime, Hedi got her piano lessons. Mother said it was worth waiting to go to a good place. She wasn't impressed with Mrs. Maxwell's Elocution Studio on 181st Street where the O'Connell twins went.

Josef Norman was a famous director in Europe before the war, and Father and Mother knew all about the work he did with Bertolt Brecht. They said it was modern theater. Mother told me about how Josef Norman had his actors come out from all over the auditorium to make the audience feel like part of the performance. He was a sensation in Vienna and Berlin. Before Hitler, of course. Josef Norman was Jewish.

It was funny—when I was younger I used to think Mother and Father actually knew all the European celebrities. It was because of the way Mother would say, "Ah, Marlene Dietrich!" or "Oh yes, Hedy Lamarr, she was Hedy Kiesler . . ." or "Of course, Josef Norman!" Later, I realized that tone of familiarity was because it was a name from their Austrian life.

Mother said Josef Norman taught the Stanislavsky way. I didn't know what that meant.

"I do not know either," she said, "but if you are accepted, you will find out soon enough."

I had to go for an interview with Mr. Norman, and he accepted me!

Mother studied me speculatively when she got the news. "So, perhaps it is not only a daydream. You must have a real talent."

She said it seriously and with respect. I felt a burst of sunlight inside, but I kept my face normal and discussed it seriously with her, too.

"But you know," I said, "he didn't ask me to act anything. He didn't see me act at all."

"What did you do?"

"We talked. He asked me about school and about my favorite subjects and what I liked to read. Things like that."

"He was a very famous director, Liesl. He can tell."

"But how? Just by talking to me?"

159

"I am sure he could see that you are a very intelligent child," Mother said, "and able to learn."

It wasn't intelligence that I wanted. Maybe he could see talent radiating from me through my big brown eyes. I thought of Grace Flanagan and how she used to sing, with her face lighting up and something magical happening.

I went to the first class at the studio on a Thursday afternoon, right after school, with no time to go home in between. I put some lipstick on and combed my hair in the cracked mirror of the gum machine while I was waiting for the subway.

The entrance for Alder-Norman was past the box-office part of Carnegie Hall, where the concerts were, but it was not an ordinary office building. I could hear drifts of piano music while the elevator was going up, and the floor just below said "Ballet Arts." It was a building full of musicians and dancers and actors. I was going to be one of them. I had read somewhere that great stars carried their own spotlights around inside them, and I could almost feel my own special beam of light. The celebrity I needed to be was going to be born now. It would be a moment to remember: the elevator gate squeaking open, the wrinkled elevator operator in a blue-gray uniform, a faint smell of rosin, my first step into the Alder-Norman Studio and into another world.

There was another moment that I remembered. It went by in an instant, but the scene stayed with me ever after. I was much younger then and I had been walking on the sidewalk of St. Nicholas Avenue when a long white convertible pulled up and parked at the curb. There were some men in the car, but my focus was on the beautiful, golden-tanned woman in the front seat, smiling with very white teeth and glistening red lips, a soft white coat loosely draped over her shoulders. She was too glamorous and extraordinary to possibly belong in Washington Heights. She, the car, everything about her, was totally out of place. She looked around at the street and smiled and said something to the men and smiled some more. Then the car drove off. It happened so quickly and I thought about it so much afterward that it took on the feeling of a dream. I thought she had lived in Washington Heights long ago and then became a star and had come back just to look at the street where she had once been ordinary. I was sure that was why the car had stopped that way. I could see that scene and myself on the sidewalk, ten years old, looking at her in awe. But now I was entering the Alder-Norman Studio and I saw it like a mirage and the woman in the car was me, all grown up, glancing past a little girl on the sidewalk. I would be a star like that, and I already felt the loss of what I was leaving behind—Grace Flanagan, Teresa, Olivia, and the streets of Washington Heights where I wouldn't fit in anymore. Maybe I wouldn't have to leave Billy Laramie behind. He was handsome enough to be a movie star with me.

The anteroom of Alder-Norman had thick green wall-to-wall carpeting, which made everything very hushed. My footsteps were silent. There were framed photographs of actors on the walls. I didn't recognize any of them. They were probably Broadway actors and not that famous. There was a big picture of Josef Norman with another man. Mr. Norman wouldn't be teaching me himself because he didn't take the younger classes.

My teacher would be Grant Hayward. I had read about him in the catalogue. It said he was an actor on stage and screen, but I didn't recognize his picture either. I thought of getting his autograph, but I knew it would be the wrong thing to do. I was going to be an actress, too. Colleagues didn't ask each other for autographs.

I was supposed to go to Room 2, and I left the anteroom and the thick carpeting turned into black-and-white linoleum. Room 2 was small and bare except for a lot of folding chairs. The only pattern was from the linoleum. I recognized Grant Hayward though he wasn't as young as his photograph. He said to call him Grant because this wasn't like school. He wore a white shirt and his fingernails had colorless polish and were cut perfectly evenly. He looked immaculate, and next time I'd be sure to wash my hands very carefully before I left school.

The other kids in the class didn't look special in any way. There were five girls and two boys. I opened up one of the folding chairs to sit down and it made a lot of noise. Something got stuck and it took me a long time to get it open all the way and the other kids silently watched me struggling with it.

"You'll get to know each other very well," Grant said, "but for now, start off by telling each other your names and where you live."

"Ann Liebman, Forest Hills."

"Norine Smith, Manhattan."

I looked around at the girls. No one was that pretty. I had thought they'd all be beautiful if they were going to be actresses.

"Sam Denning, Manhattan."

He was heavy, with chins and a thick neck. He looked like a young Charles Laughton. I wondered if it was possible to be a teenage character actor.

"Jeannette Conklin, Brooklyn."

"Francine Klein, Manhattan."

"Tommy Grace, Queens." He looked young, younger than thirteen.

"Gloria Landis, Staten Island."

"Lisa Rosen, Washington Heights." My voice came out breathless. I sounded nervous. I had planned to speak clearly, in nice, rich tones.

"Okay. Everybody, pull your chairs around in a circle," Grant said. He waited until the scraping of chairs on the floor ended. We were all quiet and waiting.

He laughed. "You're all so tense. I can feel your

tension crackling in the air."

We looked around at one another and some of the kids smiled. We were all holding blue soft-cover books that said "Samuel French." The books were given to us when we registered, and we were each supposed to have memorized one of the monologues in them. I'd memorized mine perfectly, word for word. All week, I had made Hedi or Mother or Father hold the book for me whenever I could catch them.

Grant was talking. "You're going to do your scenes in a little while, and because this is the first class, you're feeling nervous. That's okay. You're going to learn to control that nervousness and use it and turn it into performing energy. Suppose you're crossing a busy street and you're in the middle and a car is coming right at you. If your fear makes you stand still, paralyzed, in the path of the car, you'll get killed and that's bad. If your fear gives you that extra burst of adrenaline and you run faster than you ever knew you could, you get out of the way of the car, you've used your fear to your advantage, and that's good. When an actor goes onstage without some of that fear or tension, then he'll have no energy in his performance. Think about it and learn to use it.

"There are tricks to calm yourself. All right. Both feet. Take your toes and scrape them along the bottoms of your shoes and concentrate on localizing your tension there. Try it—it might work for you."

I tried to scrape my toes against my soles. There

wasn't much room to do it in. I was wearing my penny loafers with brand-new shiny pennies in them for luck. They glinted as my toes wiggled. The girl next to me, Francine something, was frowning with effort. Her shoes were moving, too.

"Acting can't begin until you lose your self-consciousness. The way to do it is through concentration. Lose yourself in your character. Who are you? Where are you? What is the emotion in your scene? Forget about impressing me or anyone else. Concentrate!"

My scene was about a queen named Mary Stuart who was locked in a dungeon. I thought dark, afraid, lonely. I looked around at the rest of the class. Everyone looked deep in thought.

"The more you forget your audience, the more you will draw them in. Don't go to them, make them come to you."

I listened to him as hard as I could. Was it possible to concentrate so hard that I would really forget all the other people sitting around and watching?

"Let's get started. First, get yourselves loose. Take your shoes off. Next time, wear your oldest, most comfortable clothes."

I had worn my favorite navy-and-red-plaid pleated skirt. I had planned what to wear to this class for days. If I was going to be an actress, I had to dress perfectly. Joan Crawford once said that a movie star was obligated to always look like one, even when grocery shopping. I thought I was entering this beautiful new world, and now he wanted us to wear old clothes!

"Everybody, get up." Eight chairs scraped back. "Stretch, touch your toes, shake your arms and legs, loosen all the kinks. Yawn! Bigger yawns! Francine, you can make it bigger than that. Come on, Lisa, stretch that jaw. Arms up. Reach up to the ceiling. Sam, reach! Now hang down and relax."

It wasn't until after we did the stretches that I realized that my arms had been tight with tension.

We started into the scenes. Norine was first, and I wondered how she could concentrate with Grant staring so hard at her.

Norine was about my age, plain, with freckles on pale white skin. Her monologue was from *Seventeen*, by Booth Tarkington, and I hadn't understood it at all when I read through it at home. I had thought it was some strange Southern dialect. When she did it, I realized it was supposed to be baby talk and the character was supposed to be very cute and flirtatious. Norine's voice purred and the change was amazing. She was coquette and charming and . . . even pretty! She was wheedling and feminine and she was wonderful in that scene! I was glad I didn't get that one to do. I couldn't have done it nearly as well.

She sat down and she was plain Norine again. Grant said a lot of things about gestures and mannerisms, and I couldn't understand what there was to criticize, because she had been wonderful! We were all supposed to be listening, but I was up next and I was too busy thinking. I wanted so badly to be good, too.

When it was my turn, I knew the words perfectly. I even shivered because I thought it would be cold in the dungeon. I thought I did it pretty well. I did it better for the bathroom mirror at home, though. I finished and looked at Grant and waited for his comments.

"That's not bad, Lisa," he said. "You were shivering. Why?"

"It's supposed to be a dungeon. I thought it would be cold."

"Were you cold, Lisa?"

What did he mean? The radiator on the side of the room was hissing. "Me, personally? No."

"You were pretending to shiver, Lisa, and it was phony. Acting is not pretending. Acting is *being*. I want everything you do to come from the inside out. Let the action and the words follow the feeling. Lisa, don't try so hard. Let it happen."

While the other scenes went on, I thought about that. How could I help trying so hard when I wanted so badly to be good? Did he mean that I really had to be cold before I shivered?

"Time's up. You all did fine for the first session. I probably threw you a curve, having you do a scene without working on technique first, but I wanted to see what we were starting with. Next week we'll be doing improvisations and . . ."

I heard snatches of conversation from the other kids

as we left the room.

". . . casting at Macy's. For the Easter show . . ."

"I got a callback for the . . ."

"I just started at Professional Children's School and . . ."

"So long. See you next week."

It was already rush hour when I got into the subway. I was jammed between people. I felt wooden. I had thought shivering was such a good idea and he hadn't liked it at all. Thinking up things like that was what had made me the best actress in school. I had always tried to think of an extra thing like that, and now Grant said it was phony and I didn't know what to do.

Maybe I had gotten all those parts in school because I was supposed to be smart and the teachers knew I could memorize. I could memorize faster than anybody. But memorization had nothing to do with what Norine had done in that scene.

I got a seat on 125th Street and I sank into it. I was suddenly so tired and my legs ached. How could I stop trying too hard? And what if I turned out to be ordinary, if I didn't have talent?

I had hated it when he made us do big yawns. I had felt my jaw relax, but I had felt ugly and I hoped the fillings in my back teeth didn't show. I couldn't imagine them doing big, grotesque yawns on the Metro-Goldwyn-Mayer lot.

Norine was so much better than me, and so was that

boy, Sam, who did the Stage Manager in *Our Town*. That special beam of light inside me felt extinguished.

Next week I'd wash my hands before class and I'd be immaculate and I'd study my scene carefully. I couldn't give up. "Let it happen," he'd said. How? And in the meantime, I'd have to come into the house looking happy and excited for Mother and Father and Hedi instead of as limp as I felt. That would be real acting.

16

It was Saturday night and I was at Olivia's house, because Larry Cramer and Kenneth Weiss were going to pick us up there. Olivia was going to be with Larry Cramer, of course, and Larry had told her that Kenneth liked me and they set the whole thing up. Kenneth was Larry's friend and one of the more grown-up boys in Rapid Advance.

"You know something?" I said. "I've never said two words to him, so why should he like me?"

"Oh, Lisa, he just does, and don't you think he's cute-looking?"

"No."

"Oh, he is so. He's the second-cutest boy in the class after Larry."

I didn't think Larry was cute, either, but I couldn't tell Olivia that. I was going because Olivia and I were best friends and Larry and Kenneth were best friends and Olivia kept asking me. The main reason, though, was that I had never had a real date. I had to give up on Billy Laramie, and thirteen seemed like an overdue time for my First Date. I'd die if Kenneth knew. I'd try to do everything right the way *Modern Screen* said, so he'd think I'd been on lots of dates before. *Modern Screen* said to talk about what the boy was interested in, so I had forced myself to read the sports pages in yesterday's *New York Times*. And I'd ask him lots of questions and be a good listener, just like I was supposed to.

"They'll be here in a minute," Olivia said. "Do I look all right?"

"You look great," I said.

Olivia and I had spent the afternoon setting each other's hair in pageboys. It seemed strange to go to so much trouble, because Larry and Kenneth saw us every single day in school looking normal.

When the doorbell rang, it echoed all through Olivia's apartment and made me jump. We were in Olivia's room, standing in front of the closed door, and we could hear Olivia's mother opening the front door and we could hear their voices in the living room. We watched the alarm clock on Olivia's dresser. We were supposed to wait five minutes before we came out. *Modern Screen* said that if we were ready right away, we would seem too eager, but if we kept them waiting too long, it would be inconsiderate. Five minutes was

171

just about right.

Olivia put some Lily of the Valley on her earlobes and handed it to me and I put it on, too.

I was glad I was being picked up at Olivia's. I was glad it was Olivia's mother out there talking to them. I couldn't trust Mother or Father to handle it the right way, because I didn't know how they did it in Europe. Maybe Father would ask too many questions. Maybe Mother would call and tell me to hurry up and not understand about waiting five minutes. And Hedi would probably make fun of me later.

"Lisa, it's time," Olivia whispered.

"Oh. All right." I caught my breath.

"Okay?"

"Okay," I said.

We came out into the living room and it was almost a surprise to see that all this trouble was for Kenneth Weiss, second row from the back in homeroom, Kenneth Weiss who was exactly my height and had big ears.

On the way to the RKO, I asked Kenneth which baseball team he liked and he said he never watched baseball, he just liked to play sometimes. I asked him what position and he said he played different positions and I said, "Oh." And then there was a long silence. Then I asked him if he had any hobbies and he said, "No," and I said, "Oh," again. I asked him if he liked football and he said, "Yes." How was I supposed to be a good listener if he didn't talk?

We were walking right behind Olivia and Larry.

Kenneth suddenly made a big move to get on the street side of me, as if he had just remembered he was supposed to be there, and I got the terrible feeling that it might be his First Date, too.

At the movies, Kenneth and Larry went to the ticket window and Olivia and I waited off to the side, looking every which way but in the cashier's direction. We weren't supposed to notice them paying for us. Same at the candy counter. We took the popcorn, but we looked the other way when Larry and Kenneth reached in their pockets. That's what *Modern Screen* said to do. I wondered what was so terrible about seeing money. I was getting very tired of doing all the things I was supposed to do, trying to get Kenneth to talk and smiling all the time.

It was a relief to sit down in our seats in the dark. All I would have to do now was watch the movie. Teresa had seen it and she said it was good. Later I'd tell Kenneth that I'd enjoyed it and then say "Thank you" and "Good night" and I'd be finished. And in the meantime I could relax and watch.

It had already started. It was with Barbara Stanwyck and she was a blonde for this movie. I thought she looked very good as a blonde—maybe she'd keep it that way—and then Fred MacMurray came in. He was an insurance salesman and . . .

Kenneth's arm was around my shoulder! He put it there all at once, in one big move. I looked at him and he was staring at the screen and pretending his arm wasn't even there.

I looked at Olivia, and Larry's arm was around her shoulder, too. They were talking and she was giggling.

Barbara Stanwyck was kind of half smiling, in a challenging way, and looking at Fred MacMurray from under her eyelashes, so he kissed her and the screen went dark. Then they were plotting about killing someone and . . .

Kenneth's hand felt sweaty on my shoulder. I could feel it right through my blouse and I wished he would move it away. I sat stiffly. I didn't know what to do. I couldn't tell him to take his arm away.

Now Edward G. Robinson had come into the picture and he was very suspicious. He was asking lots of questions about the killing, because he was the special investigator who . . .

Olivia and Larry were kissing right next to us!

I hoped Kenneth wouldn't notice, but he did. I could tell he did, even though he was pretending to be staring right at the screen. And I knew he would do it, too, just because Larry was.

All of a sudden, his head was blocking out Edward G. Robinson and he was kissing me. It didn't feel good or bad, especially, just weird. He was doing something with his tongue and I kept my lips closed tight and I could feel his saliva all over and I was thinking how weird it was. I was thinking about that time we went on vacation and I forgot my toothbrush and the drugstore was closed. Mother said to use Hedi's and I was shocked, I wouldn't in a million years, and here I was with this strange boy's saliva slobbering all over my mouth. We kept kissing because I was too embarrassed to push him away or say anything and that's what I was supposed to do and that's what Larry and Olivia were doing. I was listening to bits of the movie and I felt like I was stuck in flypaper and I was wondering if Kenneth was really enjoying this a lot, because I wasn't. He smelled like Lavoris mouthwash.

I finally thought of something to say.

"Hey, Kenneth," I said, "do you have any popcorn left?"

"What? Oh. Here," he said. He was breathing fast and he handed me the popcorn.

There was hardly any left, but I thought if I could just keep on eating, chewing little teeny tiny pieces carefully, I could keep it going for a long time. My neck felt stiff.

When he kissed me again, I was all buttery and salty and he was still salivating and it was the world's longest movie and I started thinking of how Billy Laramie had ruined the whole story of my life. My first kiss was supposed to have been with him and now it was this awful mess. It was all Billy Laramie's fault!

"Come on," I finally said, "let's watch the movie."

"Oh. Okay." Kenneth sounded so embarrassed that I started to feel sorry for him. We'd never be able to face each other in school on Monday.

175

I stared at the screen and tried not to be aware of Olivia and Larry. I hated Billy Laramie with all my heart.

I had stopped at the library on my way home from school and I had an armful of books. I was walking home along St. Nicholas Avenue, and at each block, I shifted the books over to the other arm. I kept wishing a bus would come. There wasn't one in sight and I didn't feel like standing and standing at the bus stop. Sometimes it took fifteen minutes for a bus to come; I could walk home by then. I kept turning around and checking behind me, just in case a bus was coming up the street. Those books were getting heavier! When I passed the 183rd Street bus stop, I turned around again and I saw Billy Laramie walking behind me. He half nodded to me and I kept on walking.

It felt dumb. I knew he was behind me and I wondered if he was watching me. I shifted the books to my other arm. I'd have to go eight more blocks with him behind me! I didn't want him making fun of the way I walked. Some of the girls at Humboldt had a sexy way of walking, hardly lifting their feet and dragging their heels. I tried it for a few steps, but my shoes dragging along the sidewalk made too much noise and made me feel even more self-conscious. So I started walking regular again.

I glanced over my shoulder to see if he was still there.

"Hi, Liesl," he said.

I didn't answer. He was always ignoring me, anyway.

I thought about crossing St. Nicholas Avenue, but then I'd have to stop and wait for the light and he'd think I was waiting for him to catch up with me.

"I said 'Hi.' You hard of hearing?"

"Oh, go jump in the lake!"

"What's the matter with you?" He was right behind me.

"Leave me alone, Laramie."

"I mean it—what are you so mad about all the time?"

I didn't say anything. I kept on walking, looking straight ahead of me.

"How come you can't say hello no more?"

"You want to know? You really and truly want to know, Laramie?"

"Yeah, I want to know."

"Okay! Some people treat other people so bad, especially when they're with some different people, and then they're too dumb to know why those other people don't want to talk to them anymore!" Saying it almost made me want to cry.

"Great goin', Rosen. That the way they teach you to talk in Rapid Advance?"

I didn't answer. It was hard to talk over my shoulder to someone behind me.

"What the hell did all that mean?"

"It meant if you're friends with someone, you don't turn it on and off and not even say hello," I said. "If you don't know me in school, don't bother me now."

"I always say hello."

"Yeah, sure. Thanks a lot."

"When don't I say hello?" he said.

I was stepping on all the cracks in the sidewalk on purpose.

"Hey, Liesl, what do you want? When I'm with somebody, I'm supposed to drop them right away just on account of you came on the scene?"

"I don't want to talk to you," I said.

"Why not? What the hell's wrong with you?"

"You want to talk, go talk to Mona."

"That time at the dance, huh?"

I couldn't answer. I just shook my head.

"How come you were there, anyway?" he asked.

What was I supposed to say? He was almost alongside.

"I never did nothing to you," he said. "You're the one that acted mean."

"Me? Me? How?"

" 'Get your filthy, rotten hands off me, you're no good, just like everybody says.' . . . Remember?"

Oh, God, he remembered it, word for word.

"That was a long time ago."

"Yeah."

"I didn't mean that, anyway," I said.

"It takes a score card to keep up with you, you know that?"

"I was a little kid then, so that doesn't count," I said.

"How come you're the one that gets to decide what counts?"

We walked along in silence for a while.

"It makes me feel damn stupid, that's all," he said. "If we're going the same way, I feel damn stupid walking three feet behind you."

"You could go across the street."

"Come on, I thought you'd grown up a little. Stop acting like a baby."

He was walking right next to me now.

A long, long silence.

"So what have you been up to? How's it goin'?" he said suddenly.

I looked at him.

He gave me that big smile that softened his face. "Hey, come on, that's normal conversation, Liesl."

"Lisa," I said. "Everyone calls me Lisa."

"Well, I always think of you as Liesl."

He thinks of me!

"So how's life treating you?" he said.

"Okay, I guess."

"Not that great, huh?"

"It's okay," I said. "I have all these books to read and a report to do."

"Let me see. What is all that stuff?" He took the books. "What is this *Honduras? The Central American States?*"

"I have to do this report on banana production. There's so much homework in Rapid Advance."

"What do you want to be in Rapid Advance for? They're a bunch of fairies."

"They're not," I said. "They're my friends."

"You know what they say. To each his own."

"My friend Olivia is nice, she's a lot of fun and—"

"I was talking about the guys."

"Oh. Well, they're nice, too, some of them. I went out with one of those boys and—"

"Oh yeah?"

"—and he was nice, too. A lot nicer than Mona, I bet. Why are you always hanging around with those Spanish Lords anyway, Billy?"

"Listen, Mona's okay. No kiddin', you'd like her if you ever got to talk to her."

"She looks like she's twenty-one or something."

"Well, she's not. She's fifteen. She's no V-girl, either."

"She looks that way."

"Where'd you get that? What'd you do, go see a V-girl movie?"

"No."

"Mona's all right. She's funny, too."

"Those Spanish Lords look like hoods. They do, Billy."

"Looks don't mean nothing. Some of them are crummy and some of them are okay, just like anybody else. I'll tell you one thing, though. If you're a Spanish Lord, they'll never let you down."

I shrugged.

"That's the truth. Like in a fight or something, they'll never let you down. Honest to God now, who could you say that about?"

"Well, my family, for one thing. I know I can count on them."

He looked at me sideways. "Yeah, maybe."

"Your family, too, Billy."

"My family? You must be kiddin'. Kate's hopin' I'll drop dead."

"I meant your father."

"Oh. Yeah."

"Is he okay and everything?"

"Oh, sure."

"The war will be over soon, that's what everyone says, so he'll be coming home soon."

"It might take him a while. . . . Anyway, the Spanish Lords are right there when you need them. And we don't do nothing so bad. You'd like some of them if you gave it a chance. You can't always go by looks, like it's some Hollywood movie. You know what I mean?"

"I guess so."

"You never know. Same with those Rapid Advance fags. Maybe I'd like them. You think so? If I got to know them?"

"I don't know. . . . I doubt it."

"Yeah, me too." He was grinning. "Well, you're Rapid Advance and I like you, so there's always a chance."

He said he liked me. And he still had my books.

Billy Laramie was actually carrying my books.

All those blocks went by too fast and we reached the building. We went in together.

We stopped in front of my apartment door. He held out my books, but when I reached for them, he didn't let go right away. Our hands brushed and a long moment went by and he was looking straight into my eyes.

"See that," he said. "We can even have a regular conversation when you watch your manners." That smile again, and then he let go and started up the stairs. "So long, Liesl."

"So long, Billy." I sounded casual. I was very careful to keep the glow out of my voice.

17

The dishes clattered as Mother finished clearing the table. We ate dinner earlier than most people because evening office hours started at six. The waiting room was full of patients and there was the slight rustle of magazine pages being turned. Father had just put on his white coat and gone into the office. Hedi was hunched over the table doing her homework, and I was curled up on the couch, reading next week's monologue. It was a quiet time. Even the shouts of the kids playing outside faded as one by one they straggled home for dinner. It was almost dark outside. It had been getting dark earlier as the days got colder. Almost everyone was home from work by now, and indoors.

"It's damn lucky I came home, you bitch!"

It was Billy's voice. I could hear him on the street,

right through the closed window.

"Yeah, Mary's been locked out since kindergarten!" Billy's voice again. "She couldn't even get in the god-damn house to pee, for Chrissake!"

An argument had spilled out onto the sidewalk in front of the building. Billy couldn't have picked a better time for a big audience.

"Don't you raise a hand to me!" That was Kate's voice.

I went to the front window and looked out from the side of the curtain. Billy was under the lamppost and Kate Laramie was a few feet away in front of the entrance.

"Where the hell you been all afternoon, huh? Tell me that!" Billy, shouting.

Hedi was at my side, looking out. "Oh boy, listen to him." She giggled.

"Why don't you mind your own business?" I said. I tried to push her away from the window and she pushed back.

"What's the matter? You're looking, too," she said.

"That's different," I said. I was sure the whole neighborhood was listening. I felt so bad for Billy. I thought I saw someone opening a window across the street.

". . . I oughtta get you declared unfit, that's what I oughtta do!"

"You're out of your mind!" Kate's voice.

"When're you turnin' pro, Kate? How come you're

givin' it away?"

"Shut up! Shut your big mouth!"

"And I'm gonna write my dad and—"

"Oh, sure. He's a big help!"

"Yeah, you'll see. Wait and see!" Billy's voice sounded hoarse. "He'll kick you outa here so fast . . ."

Some of Kate's words were unintelligible now. ". . . running wild . . . drinking beer with that spick gang . . . damn lunatic . . ." I saw her turn and go back into the building.

"Bitch!"

He was all alone on the sidewalk, in the lamplight. He was yelling in the direction she had gone.

"Bitch! Whore!"

If I had stopped to think, I wouldn't have run outside. But he was all alone, going on and on in that raspy voice. I grabbed my coat and ignored Hedi's questions.

He was still shouting when I got there.

"Billy, stop." I was breathless.

"Goddamn friggin' bitch!"

I touched his arm. "Billy, don't," I said. "Everybody's listening."

He turned to me and looked at me blankly. I took my hand from his arm.

"Billy?"

"Swell," he said. "Run right up and see the show."

"Oh, cut it out, it's *me*." I could feel the eyes behind

shades and curtains riveted on us. Hedi's, too, probably. "Come on, let's take a walk or something. Come
on. Everyone's looking."

"Let 'em," he said.

"Please, Billy. Let's go."

He started to walk with me. I tried to keep my body
straight and my head up. I wanted to be out of the
streetlamp's ring of light.

We walked a few steps and then he turned back. He
cupped his hands around his mouth and yelled up at
the buildings, "Bill Laramie, broadcasting from 191st!
Tune in next week, folks!"

"Billy, come on!"

His eyes were glittering and his mouth was set in a
tight little smile. "Same time, same station!"

I pulled at him and I was relieved when he started
to walk again and we got to the corner where it was
dark.

"You heard the whole thing, huh?"

"Me and everyone else."

"Oh shit."

"What happened?"

"She left Mary all by herself, the whole goddamn
afternoon. The kid's only five years old, for Chrissake!
And then she comes waltzin' home like nothing's
wrong."

"Maybe she had to go somewhere."

"Yeah, yeah. She was with some guy. I saw her
gettin' out of the car."

"Oh."

"So I tell her off good and—"

"Everyone heard you cursing."

"It'll give 'em something to talk about—it'll do 'em good."

I thought of how much he used to mind when people talked about him, how he used to walk down the street so fast.

"She don't lift a finger for nothing. Mary's her real natural kid and you'd never know it. Know what I mean?"

I nodded.

"And my dad's in the goddamn war and look what she's doin'! I coulda killed her tonight!"

"Your dad will know what to do. She's his wife, not yours."

"I hope he throws her out. He's no middle-age creep or nothing like that, he's a good-looking guy and look what she's doin'."

"Well, maybe she—"

"Boy, I'd like to take a swing at her!"

"That wouldn't help anything."

"I get so goddamn mad!"

He was walking fast. I strained to keep up.

"Billy, slow down."

". . . and somebody's got to show her . . ."

"Maybe she really loves your dad but—"

"She's in it for the goddamn allotment, that's all."

"—but maybe she's too lonely by herself. She's so

pretty, and maybe she wants to have fun. She's too full of life to—"

"Full of life, huh? She lays around all day and eats chocolates!"

"You know how you always used to say you miss going fishing with him and all that. Maybe it's the same for her, kind of."

"What do you know? You don't know nothin' about it, so keep out of it!"

"Okay. All right."

He looked so mad and I was almost running to keep up with him. I wasn't sure if he wanted me there at all, but I followed along next to him.

"You think it's all right for her to be sleepin' around on the side? Tell it to the Marines!"

"Well, *I* wouldn't do that," I said. "I was trying to see her side of it. If *I* loved someone, I'd always be true, no matter how far away he was. I'm a one-man woman and I'd make him happy and—"

"Woman? You?"

"Listen, Billy, what makes you think you're the only one that's getting so mature? I've grown up a lot, too. I know about loving somebody."

He looked at me sideways, one eyebrow raised. "You had sex yet? With one of those Rapid Advance fags?"

"That's not what I'm talking about!"

"You waiting for some big movie star to come charging up St. Nick? True love and what else is new."

"No! If Alan Ladd came walking up to me right now, I'd tell him he was too old for me, and anyway, I don't *know* him. I'd love someone around my own age, someone I was really friends with, and it wouldn't be just for his looks, either. It wouldn't be just because his eyes are blue or something like that."

"Alan Ladd's heart will get broke for sure."

"Cut it out, Billy! You always think you know everything!"

"No I don't. I don't even know how I'm gonna get through the next day living in the same house with her."

"Well, when your dad—"

"Yeah, yeah. When my dad gets back."

We were passing Healy's Bar & Grill and his profile was silhouetted against the greenish light from Healy's window. He was looking straight ahead.

"I'm going to tell you something. He's not going to get back, not for a good long time."

"Why? What do you mean?"

"He's in the brig. See, he got in some kind of trouble, somebody he couldn't get along with. . . ." His tone was expressionless.

We passed by Healy's and his face was in dark shadows again.

"Listen, don't spread it around," he said.

"No, I won't." I started to reach out to touch his arm, but then I didn't. "I'm sorry," I said.

"It's all right. I don't hardly know him, anyway."

He was walking so fast.

"When my mother, well, you know . . . he couldn't take care of me by himself. I didn't get to live with him again until after he and Kate got married. So then he has to go and take off on me again."

"Take off?"

"He wasn't drafted or nothing. The son of a bitch had to go and join up! He had no business doing that. Son of a bitch war hero!"

He hadn't looked at me at all. I thought that if I stopped, he'd keep on going without me. We walked almost a block in silence.

"Kate can't even take care of herself. She sure don't do nothing for Mary. So what if it's only my half sister, she got a lot of personality for a little kid, right? So if I say something, Kate tells me to mind my own business, and it's the Friday night fights every damn night of the week."

There was nothing I could say. One hundred eighty-sixth Street. I wished I knew how to comfort him. One hundred eighty-fifth Street. And then, finally, he slowed down.

"Hey, Liesl . . ."

"Lisa," I said.

". . . Lisa, where are we goin' to?"

"I don't know."

"You got any money on you?"

"A quarter." It was in my coat pocket.

"I ran out without nothing. I got a dime some-place." He was feeling around in his pants pocket.

"No, nothing, dammit. No, wait, here's the dime. Listen, you want to go for coffee-and?"

"Sure," I said.

"Next time'll be my treat, okay?"

"Okay." He had said next time.

"Let's go over to the Greek's."

The luncheonette was too brightly lit. There was a large "Drink Coca-Cola" sign and the tired remnant of a cake under a speckled glass cover. There were some men sitting at the counter, but the two booths in back were empty. I sat down on the worn maroon leather. Billy went up to the counter and brought back two coffees and a prune danish. I thought he would sit down opposite me, but he said, "Slide over," so I did and he sat down next to me. I could feel his arm against mine through my coat sleeve.

He was pouring a stream of sugar from the container. "Are you gonna get in trouble with your folks for running out like that?"

I had forgotten to think about it. Father had been in the office and Mother was in the kitchen with the water running. They probably hadn't heard anything. Maybe Hedi wouldn't tell. "No, I don't think so."

"See, I always have some coffee with my sugar." He was stirring. "I wasn't looking to make a spectacle of myself."

"It wasn't that bad." It was, though. It was one more thing for the neighborhood to hold against the Laramies.

We were sitting so close to each other. I could see the little chip on his front tooth and an eyelash that had fallen off and was resting on his cheekbone.

"Come on, have a bite of this danish," he said.

"That's okay, you have it." I put down the impulse to brush off the wayward eyelash.

"Hey, come on, it's your quarter."

"No thanks, I don't want any, really." The blue of his eyes, close up, was brilliant. I felt seared, as if I were staring straight up into the sun. Oh, Billy!

"Okay." He took a big bite. "You sure now?"

I nodded.

"I'm hungry. The only thing in the goddamn house was pretzels." Another big bite, and then, looking straight at me: "How come you came running out like that, Liesl?"

No one outside the family ever called me Liesl anymore. It warmed me and I didn't correct him this time.

"It hurt me to see you yelling like that, you know, in front of everybody."

"It did? . . . I kinda lose my temper now and then." Big grin, and I was surprised by his fast change of mood. I was still thinking about the fishing, ball-playing, father-and-son stories he had always told me.

I hesitated. "And I thought you might want to be with someone. I mean, to talk to."

"You're easy to talk to, you know that?"

"You always said I talked too much."

"You always did. So what? You were never boring."

He gave me his full smile. I'd forget how his smile could light up his whole face until I saw it happen again.

He took a sip of coffee. "I been thinking about what you said the other day."

"What?"

"Remember what you said, about not saying hello in school?"

"Oh, that."

"Did you mind? I didn't think you'd care."

"Of course I did."

"You cared, huh?"

"Yes."

"I been thinking about it. I'm with this big crowd, see, and you don't know any of the girls or anything. What am I supposed to do? I hang out with them. I can't walk away just like that. . . . I always said hello."

"You acted like you didn't even know me, Billy."

"No I didn't."

"I always thought we were friends and you acted like—"

"We are friends," he said. His voice had become very soft. "When weren't we friends? Come on, when?"

His mouth was inches from mine. He smelled of cigarettes and coffee and there was a tiny scar on his upper lip that I had never noticed before.

"Oh, Billy!" I said, and my own voice startled me, because I didn't know I was going to say it out loud.

The men at the counter were arguing, something about politics, and Billy put his arm around me and his hand was firmly on my shoulder. One of the men kept saying something about General Charles de Gaulle and there were long, sweet trumpet sounds from the jukebox and Billy's lips first just grazed mine and then settled into a real kiss.

I had thought so long and so hard about kissing Billy Laramie. I had practiced against the doorframe when I was little, pretending it was Billy Laramie. And now it was happening, with warm lips and real flesh and his arm tight around my shoulders. It was all different from imagining it, but it was mixed up with years of daydreaming, too. I reached for his hand on the table and it was real, rough and chapped.

"So what do you think? This mean we're gonna be friends?" His smile melted everything for miles around.

I couldn't find my voice. "I think that's what it means." It came out a husky whisper.

I watched him finishing his coffee. The men at the counter were still arguing. Their loud voices, the jukebox wail of Harry James's trumpet, the grease smell of hamburgers on the grill became mixed up with Billy's eyes looking at me over a thick white china cup and my fierce, sharp happiness.

18

I knew that Grant Hayward was a wonderful teacher. There were so many things about acting that he wanted us to understand.

We did pantomimes and he wouldn't let us fake anything. We couldn't casually pretend to be washing up. We had to remember exactly how it felt: water on our hands, the slipperiness of the soap, toothbrush bristles against our gums. We did improvisations and we worked on our diction. We recited the alphabet in a range of emotions, and we were teamed into pairs (I was with Norine) and became mirror images of each other to train our powers of observation.

He talked about typecasting and about how real actors could become a variety of personalities. I thought about that a lot. I was at my best in a mono-logue about a lost shepherdess. Grant said I had a nice quality of vulnerability. Sometimes I felt that was all I had, and sometimes it was like coming up against a wall when I tried to do something else. And sometimes . . . well, I was almost bored. When we had to lie on the floor and think ourselves into a hot bath, Norine's face actually became flushed from the steam. I felt the hardness of the floor and became . . . bored. But I went faithfully every Thursday afternoon, though that meant not being with Billy.

I was Billy Laramie's girl friend now! The kiss at the Greek's luncheonette had started everything and we met after school. We necked a lot and Billy put his tongue inside my mouth. Grace and Teresa used to say that French kissing was bad because it meant all kinds of other stuff. We all said that we'd never let anyone do that to us, but it was different now because it was Billy and me.

We necked behind the rocks in Fort Tryon Park until a whole bunch of little kids playing hide-and-seek turned up. We necked up on the roof, between clotheslines, and hoped nobody would come up to hang laundry. We spent an afternoon not seeing *Going My Way* in the dark, smoky balcony of the RKO Coliseum. Billy's fingers on the back of my neck sent prickles down my spine. Billy's hands bunched up my clothing and I'd get all those feelings.

It was fall edging toward winter. The air felt like a bite of crisp, cold apple. We walked a lot, looking for someplace to go. We walked along the Harlem River, down near High Bridge, talking about ourselves. He liked to hear about the big crush I had on him when I was little. I could tell by the pleased and sheepish way he smiled.

"You liked me that much? Honest to God?"

"I thought you were the best-looking boy I'd ever seen."

"No kidding? You did?"

"I always liked you so much!"

He thought my eyes were beautiful. He said so. He liked my gardenia perfume. I knew it was real love. There was a test in one of the magazines to tell if it was love or only infatuation. Billy and me was love, because we had known each other for so long and we got a lot of extra points for that, even though we didn't share any hobbies. I was sorry we didn't, because that would have given us five more points. I couldn't think of any hobby of Billy's and I wasn't that sure of what he did when he wasn't with me. I'd hear bits of things about the Spanish Lords, about rumbles and other gangs and drinking beer, but that wasn't the sort of thing the magazine had in mind. I didn't have a hobby either. Drama classes at Alder-Norman were too serious to be called a hobby.

One of the very serious classes was the one about sense memory. Grant said it was important.

"The basic emotions are universal," Grant said. "Every member of the audience has felt fear, anger, joy, and so on, and if you are able to convey those feelings truthfully, they will immediately identify and respond. They will just as immediately pick up any false notes. So—your job is to *feel* the appropriate emotion in a scene. I am not talking about some vague mood. I want the raw, immediate emotion. Okay so far? Okay.

"You can re-experience a feeling through sense memory. Thinking about an incident is not enough. True emotional memory lies only in the senses. Forget your intellect now. Concentrate on the senses: sight, sound, smell, taste, touch. Everybody, pick an incident that made you unhappy, that drew tears. No one will know what it was. You will answer my questions only in terms of the senses. Sight, sound, smell, taste, touch. Think of something more than two years old. Anyone ready?"

Sam was first and I listened.

Grant: All right, smell. Were there any odors around you?

Sam: Ah . . . a kind of salty, fishy smell. And a . . . I don't know . . . like something freshly washed, a kind of soapy smell?

Grant: Concentrate on those odors. Smell them now. How about sounds? What did you hear?

Sam: Voices. Loud voices.

Grant: High or low? What kind of voices?

Sam: Both, men's and women's. Especially a woman's voice, very loud and shrill.

Grant: Hear it now. Sight. Was it night or day,

indoor lighting or . . .

Sam: Day. Very bright sunlight. Squinting in the sun.

Grant: Any colors?

Sam: A yellow-and-white-striped awning and . . .

I had to think of an incident. Grant wanted something sad. Something that would bring tears. Something from long ago.

I understood what he meant about sense memory. I'd be sitting in school or lying in bed at night and I could replay Billy's words over and over in my mind, hearing the exact sound of his voice. The way Billy had said, "Hey, I guess we're boyfriend and girl friend now." I'd think about the warm, moist way his lips felt or his tongue licking my ear, and those feelings would come up so strong that I was almost in pain. But that wasn't something sad or from long ago. . . .

Sam had finished and looked shaken. His lips were pressed together tight.

"Don't hold anything back," Grant said quietly.

"I'll try." Sam's voice was breaking and he seemed to be fighting hard to hold back tears. I wondered what the memory was that he had evoked. It must have been very bad.

"Do your scene with me," Grant said. "Right now. . . ."

It was a scene about a boy trapped in a coal mine. Grant was the voice of the rescuer up above, trying to reach him, and Sam was the trapped boy, giving up hope. He started the lines with that same holding-back-tears feeling and then, in the middle part, where he talks about all the things he'll never see again or get to do, Sam started to really cry, with real tears, and it was the best thing he'd ever done in class. It was so good! There was a long silence when he finished and then we all started to applaud, and there was never applause for class exercises! Sam was beginning to smile a little, but I could see that it was hard for him to pull himself together, even now that the scene was over.

"Excellent!" Grant said. "That was true and honest. You see how it works? Who's ready? Okay, Norine, you're on next."

"But if you're about to go on in a play," Tommy said, "there isn't time to do all that. I mean, if you're backstage, waiting to go on . . ."

"The next time Sam does the coal mine scene, certain words will most probably trigger the tears. You become conditioned in rehearsal, and by the time you get to performance it's almost a reflex action. The more you use sense memory, the more quickly it will come, and you won't need anyone to lead you through it. All right, Norine. Let's do it. Was there an odor or fragrance of any sort?"

Norine was describing the odor of wilted roses and her lips were trembling already.

I had to think of an incident to use. Even if he didn't get to me until next week, I had to think of something when I cried. Something from long ago. That would have to be in Vienna. But I had never cried when I heard the grown-ups talk about the terrible things— Levine's shop windows broken, the synagogue on Taborstrasse in flames, the knock on the Mayers' door in the middle of the night . . . I would listen, standing very still, a large hollow expanding in my chest.

No, I couldn't use those things just to improve some monologue! It would have to be something simpler. Something that allowed tears.

I cried when we left Mitzi with the neighbors (the nice ones who continued to greet us, even after Hitler). She was a timid and gentle cat, and she was most especially mine, more than Hedi's. It was hard enough for humans to get into the United States—we couldn't bring an animal. What were the sights, sounds, smells when we left her behind? Touch: soft, warm fur and the smooth feeding dish, smooth except for the chipped part at the bottom. Smell: the faint smell of oatmeal from breakfast, some burned-on parts left on the pot on the stove. Sight: gray fur with symmetrical stripes. Red. The feeding dish was red. . . . Where was she now? Had the neighbors taken care of her? No one wants someone else's full-grown cat. Sound. What were the sounds . . . ? Did they get rid of her after we were gone? It wasn't my fault! I had to understand, we couldn't bring an animal. . . . I had to concentrate on sound. What sounds . . .

I didn't want to do this! I didn't like rooting around

in old memories, scratching at wounds, making them bleed again. Being an actress meant being beautiful and happy. I wanted to be like Rita Hayworth in *Cover Girl*, titian-haired, dazzling in Technicolor, dancing with a radiant smile.

I stayed behind after class to talk to Grant.

"Yes, Lisa?" he said.

"About sense memory . . ." I started. "Do they use that for the movies? Would stars like Rita Hayworth need to do that, do you think?"

"I don't know," he said. "It depends. There are actors and there are personalities. Many stars are personalities who play themselves over and over again. They are fascinating and they fill up the screen with their special aura, but they are not *actors*. An actor uses technique to create a variety of parts, and the sense memory exercise is one of many techniques. Do you see the difference between a personality and a real *actor*?"

I nodded.

The awful truth was that I wasn't sure I wanted to be that kind of actor at all. I had wanted to be a movie star with my footprints immortalized at Grauman's Chinese and my picture on a giant billboard in Times Square. I had wanted to be interviewed by *Modern Screen* and go to El Morocco and sign autographs "Sincerely yours, Flame Flynn." The old daydream. I wasn't that good an actress. I was nowhere near Norine and Sam, and I wasn't sure I wanted to work that hard.

The closest I felt to being a movie star wasn't in the Thursday afternoon drama class at all. It was with Billy. Sometimes he looked and looked at me and I knew he saw something so special in me and it made my heart turn over. We were living out our own love story, just like in the movies. In many ways the movies were a lie, though. I smoked my first cigarette with Billy and I didn't cough, choke, or throw up the way Andy Hardy did. It didn't taste that bad and I kind of liked it. And I wasn't anything like the typical teenager in *Junior Miss*, where a kiss good night was enough. It wasn't nearly enough. Each time we stopped necking, it was unbearable to wait for the next time, because something always felt unfinished. We kept inching further and further, like Billy's hand under my blouse, and with each new step there was no going back. The next time we were together, we would zero in on the new move right away. I could have been with Billy that afternoon. What would we be doing now?

Sense memories. My breath came fast just thinking about it and I felt all slippery and wet and sometimes I wondered if I was a nymphomaniac. I had asked Olivia about nymphomaniacs. She said they needed to go all the way all the time and would even accost strangers in the subway because they needed it so bad. I was relieved because that wasn't me; we weren't anywhere near all the way yet, and I'd never talk to a stranger in the subway.

I wondered about a lot of things like that. I had

learned just about everything else from the movies, but with sex I was on my own. The screen went black just when the important things started happening, so I had to invent my own style. Mother had told me the facts of life about fertilization and ovulation and all that, but that wasn't sex, and sex was what was happening between Billy and me.

It was love, too, because I loved Billy Laramie. There was something so achingly alone about him sometimes, about the defiant tilt of his chin when he walked down the street all by himself. He needed me to care about him. He said never to leave him and I said I would never let him down. It was dialogue worthy of Alan Ladd and Veronica Lake, but it was happening to me!

An afternoon with Billy was better than digging out tears in drama class.

19

I was coming around the corner from St. Nicholas Avenue and I could see that something had happened from all the way up the block. There were little knots of people gathered in front of the building. It had been like that when the youngest Dwyer girl was bitten by a stray dog, when the grocery store was held up and everyone said the neighborhood was going straight downhill, when the junkman's horse collapsed on Wadsworth Avenue and someone poured whiskey from a bottle into its mouth. I didn't want anything bad to have happened, but it was interesting to have something break the monotony of the neighborhood. I hurried down the block to get in on the excitement.

I saw Ann-Marie, who used to be in my second-grade class at 189 before she switched to Catholic school.

"What's going on?" I said.

"Oh, hi, Lisa. It's those Laramies again. You missed the whole thing, though."

"What happened?"

"It's that Billy Laramie. He's in trouble again."

"Billy? What happened to Billy?" I felt the panic start to rise.

"They got into another fight, him and Kate, and this time he socked her. You should of seen her. She came screaming out of the house and her eye was swelling up and she called the cops!"

"Where is he? Where's Billy?"

Ann-Marie shrugged.

"Ann-Marie! Where is he? Did they take him . . . ?"

"No. I don't know. There was a lot of screaming and yelling and then he went down that way. She didn't call the cops until after. Mrs. Monahan told her . . . You should of seen . . ."

Ann-Marie had pointed downtown on Wadsworth Avenue. It was all over. There was no sign of Kate and the small groups were beginning to disperse. Billy could be anywhere. I couldn't stand still, but I couldn't go running off in all directions, either. I didn't know where to look for him.

Later, I watched the street out of the front window until Mother called me to dinner. She had to call me twice, and Father said the lentil soup was getting cold, and everyone got mad at me. After dinner I stayed at my post at the window. I watched the street through the sheer white curtains. It was too dark to see anyone except under the lamppost, but I didn't know what else to do.

There was no sign of him.

I kept waking up during the night. I was listening. I thought I heard something hit my window and I jumped up to look, but there was no one there. He had done that once, called me during the night by throwing pebbles at my window. But this time, in the cold gray light of almost dawn, the street was deserted.

He wasn't in school the next day or the next.

I finally went up to the third floor to see Kate Laramie. I didn't know who else to ask and I had to find out where he was.

When Kate answered the door, I was shocked. It wasn't the swelling of the eye so much. What made me cringe was the red clot near the pupil, where it should have been white. There was a purple lump on her cheekbone. She looked bad. She had been hit more than once. I felt ashamed.

"Oh. Hello." She tried to smile under the bruises. It looked as if it hurt to form her lips into a smile. "Mary's not home now. She's out playing."

Mary? She thought I had come up for Mary. It was hard to ask. I felt ashamed.

"Mrs. Laramie, do you know where Billy is?"

The smile faded. "No."

"I'm sorry." I was almost whispering. "I wanted to see him. . . ."

She looked at me hard and my eyes dropped.

"I don't know where he went," she said finally. "He hasn't been back."

"Oh," I said. "Thanks, anyway." I couldn't look straight at her. "I'm sorry."

I remembered the fight with John McIntyre and the bleeding and the way Billy had kept automatically, unthinkingly pounding him. Kate's skin looked soft and delicate in contrast to the bruises.

She half shrugged and closed the door. The cringing feeling stayed with me for a long time.

Two more days went by. I went through the motions of French club and social studies discussions and talking to Olivia and coming home and washing the dishes when it was my turn. I jumped whenever the telephone rang, and it rang constantly at our house, because of patients' calls. I was tuned in to footsteps outside my window. I was waiting for Billy.

And then I saw him at the end of the school day.

"Liesl! Over here!" He was coming toward me through the crush of kids racing down the stairs and into the school yard.

"Billy!"

"I been waiting for you to come out. . . . I went and did it this time, huh?"

"But why? What happened?"

"The regular thing. We got in another fight."

"But why did you have to do that to Kate?"

"I don't know. I didn't mean to. It happened. . . . I don't know."

"Lisa!" It was Ellen, a girl in my class. She was a few feet away. "Lisa! Did you get the math assignment?"

"Yes," I called back.

"I didn't get the page numbers. I'll call you tonight, okay?"

"Okay." She waved and I automatically waved back. She was caught up in the crowd of kids on the sidewalk.

"I was so worried about you. I was half crazy," I said. "Where were you?"

"I had to stay away. I was downtown, with Garcia, you know him? I came up here to see you. . . . You were really worried about me?"

"You know I was!"

One of the Incorrigibles punched Billy on the shoulder. "Bill. Where you been, man?"

"Around," he said. "See you, Rocco." We watched him pass by and join two other boys.

"Liesl, we got to go someplace and talk."

I hesitated for just a second. It was Thursday afternoon, my afternoon at Alder-Norman. Well, I didn't like it that much, anyway. "Okay, Billy."

"Walk me over to the bridge."

"Why the bridge? What for?" The George Washington Bridge was farther west and not on the way home. It would be especially windy there. "It's too cold."

"I'll tell you on the way. Come on."

We went past the school yard. His arm was loosely around my shoulders. I put my arm around his waist and leaned against him. It was good to be with him. My hand was able to reach around him and into the pocket of his navy pea coat.

"I forgot my gloves again," I said.

"If you're so smart, how come you're always forgetting things?"

"I'm so glad to see you! What happened?"

"You cold?"

"Freezing."

"Listen, here's what happened. I heard Kate called the cops on me—"

"But that's all over now, isn't it?"

"Well, I got in a little trouble a while back, and I was kind of on probation. . . ."

"What?" There was a shiver beginning at the base of my back.

"The Spanish Lords were in this fight one time and somebody got hurt. We all got picked up and I got caught carrying a chain. . . ."

"What? Who got hurt?"

"I don't know."

"How could you hurt somebody you don't even know? How could you?" I was seeing images of Kate's face.

"It was a long time ago. Anyhow, I was on probation, and now Kate's—"

"You never told me anything!" I never thought

about the Spanish Lords, about gang fights, about
things like that. I never had a clear picture in my
mind. I never imagined Billy using a chain. . . .

"It was a long time ago."

"But why didn't you tell me?" Images of flesh being
torn by metal. I withdrew my hand from his pocket
and plunged it into my own. "Why do you have to get
into those things? Why do you have to fight and—"

"Listen, Liesl, I don't have time for this. We don't
have time to argue about it. I'm trying to tell you
something. Just listen, okay?"

I felt the cold on the bare skin above my knee socks.

"I was on probation, and now Kate's called the cops
and she won't take me back. So the court decides
where I go next."

"Where you go . . . ?"

We were within a block of the bridge. Traffic was
heavy. Bridge traffic. A loud rumble of truck wheels.
It was a blur.

"I'm taking off," he said. "I got to."

"No!"

"The way it works, I wind up in some government
home. Or maybe they'll put me with my uncle
Charlie. He got stuck with me when my mom checked
out on me. He's a son of a bitch and he won't want me
again, anyway. He's got this chicken farm in New
Jersey. Jesus, that place stank! Either way, I can't handle it. So I'm gonna leave."

"No. Don't, Billy."

"I have to. I'm better off on my own."

"You can't! You're not even sixteen yet!"

"Sure I can. I can pass for older, and there's lots of jobs in all those defense plants. I bet they take anybody. . . ."

"But where?"

"I don't know. As far west as I can get, I guess. . . . Don't look like that—it's okay. You know me. I always land on my feet."

We were up to the bridge. The wind was blowing the back of my hair and baring my neck. I put my hands deeper in my pockets and tried to keep the cold out of my sleeves.

We went a little way up the pedestrian walk and then he stopped. He took a cigarette and cupped his hands around the match. It took two tries before he could light it.

"Did you ever come up here and stand in the middle part?" he said. "You know, where they have that line? One foot in New York and one foot in New Jersey?"

"Yes," I said. "When I was little, with Grace Flanagan and her sister Peggy."

"Yeah, I guess all the kids did that. Big deal. Two states. It's funny to think I'll never be back this way, though."

I looked at him and I knew he meant what he said about leaving.

"You know something? Maybe Kate wasn't all that bad," he said. "What did I have to go and sock her for?

How come I'm always screwing up, Liesl?"

"I don't know." I really didn't. "You get too mad."

"Don't you? Don't you get mad? I've seen you."

"Not the same way. You . . . lose control."

The wind blowing off the river had a water smell. I took a drag from his cigarette and passed it back to him.

"Maybe if you talk to her," I said. "Maybe you could apologize."

"No. It's too late."

"You have to go to school, Billy. . . . You're not old enough to . . . You're . . ."

"I'm going. I'm gonna walk over to the Jersey side and hitch from there."

"You mean *now?* Right *now?* You can't!"

"Oh no? Watch me." His chin was tilted up. I saw his seventh-grade face superimposed on this leaner, harder one.

"Stay, Billy, please!"

"I got no place to stay."

"With us! Maybe you could stay with us. I'll tell my father and . . ." There was the bedroom I shared with Hedi and the living room that was also our dining room. They were always talking about getting a bigger apartment when the shortage was over, when the war was over. . . .

Billy was looking at me hopefully. Maybe he could have the couch . . . or the waiting room. . . . How could I explain about me and Billy? "I'll ask them. Wait and give me a chance to ask them, okay? Maybe . . . maybe . . ." My words sounded hollow. Everybody in the whole neighborhood talked against Billy Laramie. Mother too.

"No, it wouldn't work out," he said, after a long pause. "I'd get hauled into court and sent someplace else, anyway."

"But I could try. . . ." I was holding on to the sleeve of his jacket.

"Forget it. It won't work. You know it won't work."

"Billy, don't go!" I felt helpless. My eyes were beginning to water.

"I don't know what else to do." He leaned over the railing and looked down at the river. The Hudson was gray and churning under us. "I swear to God, Liesl, I don't know what else to do."

"Billy, I can't stand for you to go!"

He turned back to me. "You know what I been thinking? Liesl, come with me!"

"What?"

"It'll be the two of us. It'll be good that way! We'll go across the country and we'll get to see everything and . . ."

I saw Billy and me running after a freight train, Billy hopping in and pulling me up at the last minute, me and Billy sitting on the bare wooden boards with bits of hay clinging to them, the landscape whizzing past, me and Billy . . . John Garfield and Priscilla Lane.

I had never seen the inside of a freight train in my whole life. I bet John Garfield never did either. Or the screenwriter.

"Come on, it'll be an adventure. It'll be fun, Liesl! We'll make it all the way out to California, okay? That's where you always wanted to be, anyway. I bet you get a job in the movies. . . ."

He was giving me his best salesman's pitch. He was smiling and he was working hard at it. I could see how hard he was working at it. He wanted me with him that much!

". . . And you took those acting lessons, right? You got legs as good as Grable any day. . . ."

He was pushing all the right buttons. But I wasn't the fifth-grade me anymore.

". . . And I'll get a job. Hey, I can be a stunt man! Can you see me diving off a horse, taking a car over a jump, right up in the air, *whoosh!* It'll be great, we'll have fun and . . ."

It was close to twilight. The lights of the bridge suddenly went on. They were a shimmering magical chain across the dark river.

"And we'll be together all the time. It won't be kid stuff no more. We'll be like brother and sister, and mother and father, and husband and wife, and best friends, too. We'll always stick together, you and me. . . ."

I had a mother and father and sister who made me feel lovable, no matter what. Billy only had me.

"And the beaches . . . Laguna . . . Malibu . . . and we'll . . ."

Cars were whizzing past us. Some of the headlights were on. He needed me!

"We ought to get started. We got to start hitching before it gets dark. . . ."

I put my arms around him. Then my shoulders were shaking and I tasted something wet and salty. I held on to him tight. I thought we would break apart and fly off into a thousand pieces if I didn't.

"I love you, Billy!" I said. My voice was choking.

"Jesus, Liesl, don't cry."

"I won't," I said, sobbing.

"What are you cryin' for? Hey, don't."

I couldn't stop. I buried my face against the rough wool of his jacket. I couldn't stop.

"It'll be all right, you'll see. Come on. . . ."

"I can't, Billy," I sobbed.

"Sure you can. Come on. . . ."

"I can't go with you."

"You said you'd never let me down! Come on."

"I can't!"

"Why? Why can't you?"

"Because . . . because my parents bought a ticket for me for Saturday at City Center. Because I have to give my social studies report in school on Monday. Because . . ." My nose was running and I sniffed. "Because Olivia's birthday party is . . ."

He pulled away from me. He stood and looked at me.

"Billy," I sobbed, "I'm sorry."

"You weren't ever gonna let me down! You and everybody else!"

"I love you, Billy."

"You don't have the guts for nothing!"

"Not to jump off a roof."

"Yeah. I should of known! I thought I could count on you. At least you."

"I love you, Billy!"

"Yeah, yeah. Terrific, Rosen! See you around sometime."

He turned and went a few steps. He stopped and turned back. Running away alone wasn't an adventure. He looked lost. "Liesl, come with me. . . ."

I shook my head no. The tears were streaming down my cheeks and I didn't bother to wipe them anymore.

"Suit yourself!" His words exploded at me. I couldn't see his face.

I watched him walking across the George Washington Bridge.

Wait, I wanted to say. Don't go away mad. Take care of yourself. Come back for me someday. I watched him going, all alone, and his figure became smaller and smaller and blurred through my tears.

I know how it should have been. I should have called, "Wait! Wait for me! I'm coming with you!" and he would have heard my voice through all the traffic noise and wind. He would have stopped and watched me running and running across the bridge, my hair flowing behind me, and, when I was almost there, he would start running toward me, too, and we would meet and hug and he would pick me up and swing me around and we would be laughing and crying at the same time. All around us the bridge lights and the headlights would be a blur of stars and then, as the music came up . . . The End.

And then what? I wasn't in this movie. I wasn't even going to collect the cold and wind and lights for sense memory exercises. I tried hard to stop crying as I watched him disappear into the darkness on the other side.

Good-bye, Rita Hayworth.